LADY HOPE'S DASHING DEVIL

AVA STONE

Copyright © 2016 by Ava Stone

All rights reserved.

No part of this book may be reproduced in any form or by any electronic or mechanical means, including information storage and retrieval systems, without written permission from the author, except for the use of brief quotations in a book review.

❧ Created with Vellum

∽

For Leiza McArter, Christina Fashant, Kelly Snyder, Margaret Gannon, Janet Barrett, Diane Spigonardo, Michele Gardner, Jennifer Coleman, Lisa Bridges, Martina Arguijo, Sheree Doran, Mary Dieterich, Jessica Clements, Tina Hairston and Cass Dixon ~ thank you so much for the awesome suggestions and brainstorming help on this book. I am so lucky to have such amazing street team members! I don't know what I would do without you. ~ Ava

∽

CHAPTER 1

Hyde Park, Mayfair ~ May 1817

"Oh, for heaven's sakes, Jamie!" Lady Hope Post complained as she snatched the reins away from her cousin. "You drive like an old man."

James, Lord Elston, blew out an irritated breath and folded his arms across his chest as Hope navigated his matched greys around a landau and gig that had stopped for their passengers to speak to each other. "I thought you were supposed to be *docile* these days."

"Docile?" Hope cast her cousin a sidelong glance, keeping one eye on the barouche she was trying to catch. Docile wasn't such an awful word, but the way Jamie had uttered it, made it sound like the vilest of curses. It was true she wasn't quite herself these days, and she might not ever be again; but she was trying to *help* her cousin, for pity's sake. It wasn't her fault he wasn't as skillful with his phaeton as she was. "Who said I was docile these days?"

"Grace," he muttered.

Yes, that did sound like something her sister would say.

And Grace had been in a rotten mood ever since the season and her husband hunt had begun. "Well, I suppose you could have asked *Grace* to go riding with you, if you don't like the way I drive."

"*I* was supposed to be the one driving." Jamie sat forward and motioned for Hope to turn the ribbons back over to him.

The devil's chance they'd catch Miss Alice Humphreys with *Jamie* driving. Hope gestured to the girl's barouche, which was quickly approaching the Park Lane exit. "Do you want to catch up to her? Or do you want me to let *you* drive?"

"I'm a perfectly fine driver," her cousin grumbled. "And do watch out for that couple walking right there."

Hope saw them. She wasn't blind. "I am a *Post*, James Woodward. I was raised with reins in my hands."

"Yes, well, since Uncle Thomas fell to his death driving one of these things, forgive me for not being comforted by that." He sucked in a breath. "There's another couple, Hope. Do have a care."

She saw that couple too. James should have more faith in her. She was, after all, a better driver than her cousin, no matter what he said. Besides, they were finally gaining on Miss Humphreys' conveyance, and if they missed her then this little jaunt into Hyde Park would have been for naught.

Just a little further. They'd catch her for sure on Park Lane. Hope gave the greys more lead to gather speed. "You're the one who wanted to bump into Alice Humphreys."

"*Casually* bump into her," he grumbled. "I didn't want to careen into her."

Careen into her! What a completely ridiculous—

"For the love of God!" A man bellowed at the exact same moment Jamie's greys pulled onto Park Lane and the back left wheel of her cousin's phaeton collided with…something.

Blast it all!

Hope pulled back on the reins, her heart pounding like a

drum in her chest. What in the world had she hit? She jerked her gaze back over her shoulder to find another phaeton toppled onto its side. How in the world had she hit that? And how had she knocked it over?

"Are you all right?" Jamie asked, snatching the reins back from her.

"I-I think so," she began and would have said more if the sudden appearance of an angry gentleman, glaring up at them hadn't stopped the words on her tongue.

"Are you mad?" the man demanded, his dark gaze flicking from Jamie to land quite firmly on Hope. A moment later, his eyes rounded in apparent recognition. But she didn't recognize *him* in the least. "If the shaft hadn't splintered, you'd have killed my mare. Do you realize that?"

Oh, heavens! Hope's hand fluttered to her lips.

"Terribly sorry," Jamie muttered. "Completely my fault."

"Indeed it was," the man agreed, though his eyes were still quite leveled on Hope. "This isn't the Bath Road. I can't imagine what would have possessed you to race at breakneck speed. And—"

"Honestly, Baxter, it was unintentional. An accident," Jamie continued. "Send the bills for whatever repairs are required to Weston House and I'll see that they're taken care of promptly. Is your mare all right?"

The man breathed out a breath and refocused his attention on Jamie. "James Woodward?"

A ghost of a smile tipped Jamie's lips. "Thaddeus Baxter, it's been an age."

Thaddeus Baxter? Hope knew that name. At least she thought she did. She certainly knew the surname. If things had happened differently, it would have been hers by this point.

"It's Kilworth now," the man said as his eyes flicked back to Hope.

Kilworth. Just the sound of that name made Hope's heart twist so painfully she thought she might burst into tears right there. He was Henry's cousin. The *new* Earl of Kilworth. He didn't look like Henry. His hair was lighter, almost golden and his blue eyes were so dark they were almost black. Of course, that could all have been the anger that was still rolling off him in waves.

"Yes, yes," Jamie agreed good-naturedly. "I did know that. Sorry, old man."

The new Lord Kilworth nodded once and gestured back to his fallen phaeton. "I'll send the bills to Weston House once the repairs are made."

"Oh!" Jamie handed the reins back to Hope. "Let me help you right that," he said, hopping down from the bench. "Terribly sorry again."

Hope watched as Jamie and another fellow helped Lord Kilworth push his phaeton back onto its wheels. The shattered shaft aside, it didn't look all that broken, really. His lordship cast her a censorious glare, and Hope dropped her eyes back to her lap. He might be Henry's blood relation, but the man didn't possess one ounce of the charm that her late love did. Not one ounce.

"Have you lost your mind letting her drive your cattle?" Thad shifted his glare from Lady Hope Post to her inept companion. And why had she focused her attentions on *Elston* of all people? He hardly seemed her sort, not if her usual sort was the late-Henry Baxter

Elston shrugged. "She's been driving since she was in leading strings. She's a Post."

Whatever the devil that was supposed to mean. "The last thing she should be doing is driving a phaeton through the park or…splashing through the Serpentine, for that matter," he grumbled as that particular memory darted into his head. Hope Post and Henry chasing each other through the waters in the park like a pair of escaped Bedlamites.

Elston's face turned slightly red. "My cousin is more docile this year than she was last season."

She was his *cousin*. That explained why she was in Elston's company. Thad hadn't realized they were relations, not that he'd given a lot of thought to the pretty blonde, not since last season anyway. "Tell that to my phaeton," he returned.

Elston breathed out a breath.

"Thad," his friend Robert Cole began, "it's a clean break. Davies won't have a difficult time fixing it at all."

Whether it was a clean break or not wasn't the point. Beautiful as she was, Lady Hope was a reckless chit who could have killed his horse or someone else that afternoon. And Elston was an idiot to let her drive his phaeton. During their years at Harrow he'd never thought Elston was an idiot, but apparently he'd been mistaken about that. Thad glanced again at his old classmate. "Keep your eye on her if you don't want more trouble."

Elston shook his head. "She has her own brothers for that."

Brothers who failed miserably at keeping her out of trouble most of the time, but Thad bit his tongue from saying as much. After all, Lady Hope was none of his concern one way or the other, not so long as Elston paid for his phaeton repairs. He waved the man on and returned to inspecting his broken conveyance.

He sank down to his haunches to look the shaft over. Damned lucky the break was clean and that Sulis was unharmed. The damage in property and lives could have been much worse.

Robert clapped a hand to Thad's back and said, "So much for a jaunt into Hampstead today."

Thad hadn't been dying to make that trip anyway. Visiting his aunt tended to put him in a mood. And while he had a valid excuse for cancelling those plans now, he still was still shaken by the whole event. He pushed back to his feet. "Did you see how fast she was going? Damned chit could have killed herself."

Robert grinned. "I think that's what Henry liked about her. Spirited girl."

His late-cousin had the trained eye of an unrepentant rake. "I'm certain he liked something else about her all together," Thad muttered under his breath.

"Possibly," his friend agreed, obviously having heard the comment. "Pretty girl, isn't she?"

Spirited and pretty? Fairly apt descriptions of the lady, not that Thad was about to admit that to Robert. "I didn't notice," he lied. Because he *had* noticed. He'd noticed her beauty last year when he'd first seen her, laughing and splashing her way through the Serpentine after his degenerate cousin.

But, honestly, any man with eyes would have noticed how her wet walking dress had clung to her body, and the memory of her shape was still burned into Thad's memory. Bloody inconvenient, that.

Robert laughed. "If you say so."

CHAPTER 2

It was silly that a little thing like bumping into, or colliding really, with Henry's cousin could frazzle Hope's nerves. Honestly, it wasn't Henry's cousin. It was just the reminder of Henry. Of course, everything reminded her of Henry. Any emerald made her think about the earbobs he'd sent her. Any waltz made her remember what it felt like to be in his arms. And any ride through the park brought up so many different memories of him. But until today, she'd never heard anyone else use his title as their own. And that, hearing the new earl refer to himself as *Kilworth*, was like a dagger to Hope's heart.

A knock sounded at her door and Hope pushed up on her elbows, half-heartedly. "Yes?" she called.

And then her door opened and her triplet Grace stepped into Hope's chambers. A rare smile was splashed across her sister's face. "Mr. Lacy has invited us to see Romeo and Juliet in his box this evening. Isn't that grand?"

Grand was a relative term. Young love and death would do nothing to lift Hope's spirits. "I'd rather not attend, if you don't mind."

And just that quickly, Grace's smile was gone and her brow furrowed in worry. "You love Romeo and Juliet."

She had at one point. But not any longer. "It will only make me think of Henry," she said on a sigh.

"Oh, for pity's sake," Grace complained as she plopped onto to the edge of Hope's four-poster. "You didn't die with him, you know?"

Part of her had. But there was no point in saying as much. Grace had not cared for Henry, and…Well, really *no one* had cared for Henry except for Hope and no one else seemed even remotely sorry that he was gone. "Besides, you'll do better trying to get Mr. Lacy to come up to scratch, if I'm not there." Which may or may not be true. While Grace, Hope and their sister Patience were identical in appearance, Mr. Lacy only had eyes for Grace. It truly wouldn't matter who else was around.

"I despise that play," Grace complained.

"Then why did you say yes?" Hope almost laughed.

Her sister shrugged. "I thought *you*'d enjoy it. And now I have to go and sit through the miserable thing. True love and all that utter nonsense."

True love was not utter nonsense. Hope frowned at her sister. "Do you not love Mr. Lacy even a little?" Grace had, after all, decided the gentleman in question would make the perfect husband. But if she was going to spend her life with him, shouldn't she feel *something* for him?

"I like Mr. Lacy a great deal," Grace said practically. "And if I am ever successful in getting him to propose, I am certain we will be quite happy together."

She liked him, but…"Don't you want to *love* him?"

At that Grace shook her head. "That is not an emotion I want to experience," she said, and for the first time Hope noticed a sadness in her sister's voice, almost like Grace *had* loved and lost before. But Grace had never loved anyone, not that Hope knew about anyway, and they had been together nearly every day of their lives. If there had been someone, Hope would have known, wouldn't she?

"Well, I do not want to watch Romeo and Juliet kill themselves tonight. So you shall have to go without me. I've had a very trying day."

"What happened today?" her sister asked.

Hope blew out a breath and collapsed back against her pillows. "I went riding with Jamie in the park and we had a slight accident."

"Accident?" Grace echoed. "Are you all right? Is Jamie—"

"No one was harmed." Hope winced, remembering the awful experience all over again. "But I somehow toppled over Lord Kilworth's phaeton and broke his shaft."

"Lord *Kilworth*!" Grace's voice raised an octave.

"Henry's cousin." Hope closed her eyes not wanting to remember the earl's chilly stare if she could help it.

"How did you topple over his phaeton?"

Hope still wasn't sure how she'd done that. She hadn't even seen him as they'd taken that turn onto Park Lane. "I have no idea. I was trying to help Jamie catch Alice Humphreys, when—"

"What does Jaime want with Alice Humphreys?" Grace turned up her nose, matching Hope's thoughts on the matter perfectly.

"Same thing you want with Mr. Lacy. He's terrified the Duke of Danby will have a bride for him at Christmas if he doesn't find one of his own before then."

"But Alice Humphreys?" Grace snorted. "Jamie'll be an earl someday. He can do better than some upstart merchant's daughter with the personality of a rock."

Hope agreed with the nod of her head. "But for some reason he likes her. Anyway, they've quarreled about something and he was hoping if he and I went for a ride in the park that we could bump into her."

"But you bumped into Lord Kilworth instead?"

"Unfortunately," Hope agreed. "And you should have seen the way he looked at me, Grace." She shivered. "He's rather cruel, I think. He has the coolest stare of any man on Earth, and he quite definitely hated me on sight."

"No one could hate you on sight. You look like me," her sister teased and normally such a sentiment would have brought a smile to Hope's face. But not this time. Not with the memory of her encounter with the angry Lord Kilworth fresh in Hope's mind.

"Be that as it may, the man definitely despises me. I could feel it when he looked at me."

"Perhaps he was just angry you toppled his phaeton." Grace sighed. "What did Mama say? You're still alive, so—"

"Jamie took the blame." Hope shook her head. "He's paying for the damages and told Mama it was his fault."

"That was good of him," her sister said.

"I think he was afraid Mama would kill him if she knew he let me drive."

"And if she didn't, Braden or Quent would."

True enough. Both of their brothers would be furious if they ever learned the truth of the matter.

Grace collapsed onto the bed beside Hope and rested her head on her sister's shoulder. "If you don't come to the theatre with everyone tonight, what will you do?"

"Pick a tome from the library perhaps?"

Grace snorted. "You know, once upon a time, you were the most adventurous and carefree of all of us. And now you're—"

"If you say *docile*," Hope complained, "I will punch you right in the nose."

"Even if it's true?"

It was true. But that didn't mean Hope wanted to hear it. She knew she wasn't the same since Henry's death, but there was nothing she could do about that. And being reminded of it all the time didn't help matters in the least. "I am still quite adventurous. Today I even toppled over a phaeton."

∽

Thad couldn't quite believe his eyes as he looked across the theatre. Good God. What were the odds of seeing *her* twice in one day? And what was she doing with *Daniel Lacy* of all people? That bore seemed an even less likely match than Lord Elston had. In fact, it was odd to see Lacy outside of a library, honestly. One would think the theatre was too adventurous for his soul. Must be Lady Hope's influence that had dragged the man from his usual habitat.

She *did* look tortured now that he studied her. Was it the play she objected to? Or her companion? Contrarily, Lacy looked completely enamored, gazing down at the blonde next to him as though she'd personally hung the moon and each star in the sky. Thad couldn't truly blame the man. Lady Hope was stunning. Her flaxen curls framed her face, giving her an ethereal glow. And she had the most beautiful green eyes, almost like rarest emeralds one couldn't help but admire, even from afar. He could still hear her infectious giggle as she'd splashed through the Serpentine with Henry last year. And when Thad thought about her, that gleeful sound always invaded his memory. She'd sounded so genuinely happy, so warm, so very appealing. That such a delightful sound should be in any way connected to Henry was as irritating as it was memorable. Henry had been a duplicitous jackass, and the world was well rid of him. What in the world had Hope Post seen in *Henry*? And what did she see in Daniel Lacy for that matter?

The two men had to be the polar opposites of each other. Was that the appeal?

"The, uh, stage is below." Thad's brother-in-law nudged him. "Not across the way."

He glanced at his sister's husband out of the corner of his eye. "Kindly keep your own council, Lawrence." But he pulled his gaze from Lady Hope back to the stage anyway just in time to see Romeo marry Juliet and for the curtains to close as intermission began.

Thad wasn't certain what had gotten into him, but he didn't give it very much thought. He pushed out of his chair, nodded to his sister and her husband and excused himself from his box.

Patrons filled the corridor and various colors of ostrich plumes bounced above the sea of people, but Thad still spotted her, taking Daniel Lacy's arm and smiling up at him. And for some reason he couldn't explain, Thad found himself closing the distance between himself and the mismatched pair. And then he was right there and Lady Hope looked up at him as though she'd never seen him before, like she hadn't upended his phaeton outside the park that very afternoon. And something inside him snapped.

"Do be careful, Lacy, your companion is a menace."

Lady Hope's face turned a rather satisfactory shade of red. Then she gasped. "I beg your pardon?"

Lacy frowned as he looked from Thad to the blonde and then back again. "I say, Kilworth, what do you mean by saying something like that about Lady Grace?"

And then Thad's cheeks stung with embarrassment. Lady Grace? Damn it all. Lady Hope was a twin or a triplet, wasn't she? Damned idiot. He hadn't even considered that Lacy's companion wasn't Lady Hope, not when she looked exactly like her. His mouth fell open slightly as words completely escaped him.

Words did not, apparently, escape Lady Grace who sucked in a breath and narrowed her pretty green eyes on Thad. "Hope said you were cruel. She didn't say you were daft."

"What *is* going on?" Lacy asked. "Has he insulted you, my dear?"

Lady Grace's eyes could have speared Thad where he stood. "Lord Kilworth has apparently confused me with my sister, Mr. Lacy. It's Hope he's insulted, not me, not on purpose in any event."

"I see." Lacy's frown deepened though it didn't seem as though he saw at all, not as quickly as Lady Grace had done anyway. *Cruel.* She'd called him cruel, hadn't she? Or Lady Hope had called him such and her sister had merely repeated it.

"I do apologize," Thad stammered. And, truly, those were words he rarely uttered to anyone. How unfortunate to have put himself in a position where he had to say them now.

"It's my sister you owe an apology to," Lady Grace said rather loftily. "As I can quite assure you she is not a menace in the least."

Thad wasn't quite in agreement about that. For some reason the lady in question had certainly plagued his thoughts the majority of the day. Spirited and pretty. How could he think about anything else?

"I am sorry," he said again, hating the taste of those words on his lips. "Please do excuse me," he added, turning on his heel and making an escape into the sea of other theatregoers.

What the devil was wrong with him?

CHAPTER 3

"Just go talk to her." Hope sighed. Honestly, Jamie wasn't himself at all these days, and it was slightly annoying.

But her cousin shook his head, his eyes still on the willowy blonde across the ballroom. "She won't talk to me."

"Why? What did you say to her?" She tapped him on the chest until he looked down at her.

He twisted up his face. "I didn't say anything."

Clearly, he was lying. He must have said something incredibly stupid. "What did you say, Jamie? I can't help you unless you tell me."

"I didn't say anything," he protested. "I kissed her." And then he turned slightly red at the admission.

Hope's eyes widened in surprise. She had not been expecting that. "You *kissed* her?" she whispered, moving closer to her cousin.

But Jamie closed his mouth and shook his head.

Heavens. Why was he behaving so strangely? Had he attempted even more liberties than a kiss? Is that why Alice Humphreys wasn't speaking to him? What in the world had he done? "James Woodward." She folded her arms across her chest. "What did you do to that girl? Tell me right now."

Jamie's brow furrowed. "I kissed her. That's all."

That couldn't be all. "A girl does not stop speaking to a gentleman simply because he kissed her. She—"

"It was a bad kiss, Hope. Leave it alone, will you?"

A *bad* kiss? Hope's mouth fell open. Was there such a thing as a bad kiss? She'd only ever been kissed by Henry, and it hadn't been bad in the least. In fact, it had been so blindingly wonderful, she could still remember every moment of each and every kiss. What in the world made a kiss *bad*? "How was it bad?"

Jamie sagged a bit. "Please leave it alone."

"I just don't understand how it could have been bad. You have to tell me more than that."

"It was like kissing a dead fish," he said hastily. "Slimy, clammy, no feeling whatsoever."

Heavens! A dead fish. That just sounded awful. Hope turned back to look at Alice Humphreys from across the ballroom. She'd never thought the girl was terribly interesting. She was chatting with Mr. Archibald Chapman who was mind-numbingly dull in his own right. "If there was no feeling whatsoever, Jamie, then I hardly think she's the girl for you." She might, in fact, be the girl for Mr. Chapman. Two perfectly boring individuals.

"Hardly helpful," Jamie complained. "At least I know Alice."

Oh, for pity's sake. He knew lots of girls. And maybe kissing one of them wasn't like kissing a dead fish. "I hardly see why that matters."

Her cousin snorted. "When we get summoned to Danby Castle at Christmas, there is no telling who our great-uncle will have picked out for me instead. At least I know Alice."

Of all the ridiculous—

"The Earl of Kilworth and Lord Richard Cole," the Wolverlys' footman announced, and Hope's stomach knotted into a ball.

She instinctively turned toward the entrance at hearing the name. Old habits, she supposed, not that the current earl was anything like Henry. *A menace.* He'd called her a *menace*. The awful man.

Hope's breath caught in her throat when the grumpy earl met her gaze with those dark eyes of his. So she turned quickly back to her cousin, hoping no one else noticed. What had they been discussing? Oh, yes, Miss Humphreys. Dreadful topic, that.

Hope forced herself to re-focus on the matter at hand. "You know that kissing her is akin to kissing a dead fish. You can do better, Jamie. Even Grace thinks so."

"Speaking of Grace, how did she bring Lacy up to scratch?"

After Lacy thought Lord Kilworth had disparaged Grace at the theater, the man's protective instincts had taken over and he confessed that he had quite fallen for her. But Hope was not in the mood to recant anything having to do with Lord Kilworth. "No clue. She doesn't tell me everything."

Was there a way to leave the Wolverlys' ball? Normally she could get Quent to agree to abandon a ball early, but Lord Wolverly was one of his friends and the two of them had been chatting up a storm for quite some time, as had Lila and Lady Wolverly. She wouldn't get any help from either of them. She could make her way to the retiring room and hope the prickly earl left on his own accord while she was away. Or—

"My dance, I believe." Lord St. Merryn appeared before her.

It *was* his dance. A reel. Drat it all. If only there was some way to put him off or suggest he stand up with that nice Miss

Meredith Halliday who seemed to be hiding near the far window, but she had promised the reel to the man. There was nothing for it. Hope resisted the urge to blow out a breath of frustration. Escape from the Wolverlys would have to come after her reel with Lord St. Merryn.

∽

It truly wouldn't have mattered who else was in attendance, not Castlereagh, not Liverpool, not even Prinny himself. There was no one in the world who could have dragged Thad's attention away from Lady Hope, not at that moment, not with her blonde curls bouncing, not with the splash of color in her cheeks, not with the scooped bodice that kept drawing his eyes to her charms over and over as St. Merryn spun and turned her around during a reel. In all his life, he may not have ever seen anything more fascinating.

Then again, she might not even be Lady Hope. She *could* be Lady Grace or…Wasn't there another one of them? How did people tell them apart? Three stunning girls who looked identical? The lady's yellow gown swirled about her feet and Thad's mouth went a little dry. He'd—

"There's Draughton now," Robert muttered under his breath.

The Marquess of Draughton. The reason they'd come to the damned ball. The man was a veritable jackass, but he did hold sway over a contingency of other lords in Parliament. Thad glanced briefly at the man in the far corner of the room before his gaze returned to the beautiful blonde in yellow.

Which one was she? Hope who'd upended his carriage and nearly killed his favorite horse? Grace who possessed a biting tongue? Or the other one? "Does Bradenham have two sisters? Or is it three?"

"We're not here for Draughton?" Robert heaved a sigh.

"No, we are," Thad replied, though his eyes were still on the girl in yellow. "Just humor me."

"Bradenham has three sisters, triplets. One is married to a doctor in Yorkshire. One has just become betrothed to Daniel Lacy, and—"

"Which one do you think she is?" He tipped his head towards the dance floor.

"I wouldn't have any idea. Probably not the doctor's wife. I'm certain she's in Yorkshire."

"And probably not Lacy's intended," Thad mused aloud. Assuming Lady Grace was Lacy's intended, she'd probably be with her fiancé, not dancing a reel with St. Marryn. So the girl in yellow had to be Lady Hope, at least if his process of elimination was correct.

"Most likely Lady Hope," Robert agreed. "I thought you'd meant to restore the Kilworth name, not go down the same path as your cousin."

And Lady Hope had made quite a spectacle out of herself with Henry last season. It would set tongues wagging if Thad were to take an obvious interest in the girl. Still…she didn't seem quite the same as he remembered. "Didn't she have a sparkle in her eyes last year?"

A laugh escaped his friend. "I confess I have not spent an enormous amount of time inspecting Lady Hope's eyes."

Thad had really only seen her from afar last season, but that sparkle was not one he'd forgotten. "Perhaps she finds St. Marryn a bore."

"I have found him so myself from time to time."

The reel came to an end, and Thad started for the pair without giving the matter or Robert a second thought.

"Thad!" his friend called after him, but he paid the man no attention at all. His eyes were focused solely on the lady in yellow who had captured his interest ever since he'd

LADY HOPE'S DASHING DEVIL

walked into the ballroom. And in less than a moment, the lady and St. Marryn were right before him.

She appeared slightly nervous, her eyes not lifting any further than his cravat, and Thad frowned in response. How was he to judge the sparkle in her eyes if she wouldn't even look at him?

"Ah, Kilworth." St. Marryn offered his hand to Thad. "Enjoyed your speech last week. Quite impassioned."

Thad's speech to the Lords on the need to build new churches was the last thing on his mind at the moment, even if he had come this evening to discuss that very matter with Draughton. "Thank you." He forced a smile to his face. "Lady Hope, is it not?" he said in greeting, even though they had never been properly introduced, broken phaeton shafts aside.

And then she did lift her eyes to meet his. The sparkle was definitely gone. "Making certain it's me before you warn Lord St. Marryn that I'm a menace?"

Thad's jaw tightened. He supposed he shouldn't have been surprised that Lady Grace had told her sister about their encounter at the theatre. However, it was still unfortunate that she had. He supposed he owed Lady Hope an apology, which was more than frustrating; but he'd be damned if he was to do so in front of St. Marryn.

The first chords of a waltz began and, "Would you care to stand up with me?" flew out of Thad's mouth before he could stop the words. Though it wasn't an awful idea. In fact, he might enjoy holding the girl in his arms. There was something about her.

Lady Hope, however, looked at him as though he'd sprouted horns and a forked tail. "I was just heading to the retiring room, my lord."

Well, that was poor timing. "I had hoped to speak with you about your ride in the park the other day." And apologize

19

for his comment to her sister, not that he'd say that bit out loud for St. Marryn to hear.

Lady Hope's cheeks flushed with embarrassment. "I suppose we could take a turn about the room," she clipped out.

Beggars couldn't be choosers. A turn about the room was better than her escaping to the retiring room. Thad smiled and offered her his arm, which she begrudgingly took.

"Looking forward to your next speech." St. Marryn nodded in farewell. "And you can count on my support—not nearly enough churches in Manchester."

"I appreciate that," Thad said, tucking his hand over Lady Hope's and starting for the far side of the room.

"Jamie's already offered to pay your repairs," the lady began petulantly. "So I can't imagine what else you could possibly want."

He cast her a sidelong glance, finding her eyes downcast as though watching her steps carefully. She was a dichotomy. How was this lady the same as the one who had splashed through the Serpentine and driven that phaeton with abandon? Was she the same? Had one or both of her sisters participated in those other activities? "You were the one driving that phaeton, were you not?"

Her gaze did shoot up to his then. "Are you trying to blackmail me?" she whispered.

Blackmail her? What the devil? Thad stopped in his tracks. "I beg your pardon?" There were a great number of things he'd been accused of in his life, but blackmail had never been one of them.

Her green eyes did have a bit of fire in them now, but still not that sparkle he'd once seen. "What do you want?" she ground out.

"What do I *want*?" he echoed.

LADY HOPE'S DASHING DEVIL

Her eyes narrowed perceptibly. "To keep quiet that I was driving. What do you want?"

Thad's mouth dropped open. That was truly the last thing he expected to her to say. Would she be in a heap of trouble if Bradenham or Lord Quentin found out she'd been driving? He'd always thought her brothers seemed lax, honestly. "What are you offering?" he asked, though he had no idea why he'd done so. He truly wasn't a blackmailer. But he couldn't help but wonder what the captivating beauty might offer in return for his silence.

Her nose scrunched up. "It's not supposed to work that way."

Thad shrugged, enjoying himself immensely. "Well, I've never blackmailed anyone before. How am I supposed to go about it, my lady?"

"You're supposed to tell me what you want, and then I decide if I am able to pay the price or not."

"Have you much experience with blackmailing?" he asked.

At that, a smile tipped the corners of her mouth. "I have two sisters, my lord. We have been negotiating with each other nearly all of our lives."

"Negotiating." He nodded, and started leading her around the edge of the ballroom once again. "A much nicer term than blackmail, don't you think?"

"I suppose it depends on whether you are the blackmailer or the blackmailee. Negotiation seems nicer if one is the blackmailer; but blackmail seems more apt if one is the blackmailee."

He couldn't help it, he laughed. She might not have the same sparkle in her eye that she once had, but she was the most enchanting girl he'd ever encountered. Damn Henry in his grave for finding her first.

Draughton caught Thad's eye and his laugh died away. He

did have business to attend to, no matter that he'd rather chat with Lady Hope the rest of the evening. He drew her to a stop once more. "Why don't I come by Post House tomorrow and we can negotiate further?"

She frowned slightly. "I don't know if that's the best idea."

On the contrary, it was the best one he'd had all evening. "We'll go for a ride in the park. *I'll* drive." Then he lifted her gloved hand to his lips and bowed slightly. "Until tomorrow."

CHAPTER 4

"And then he left you in the middle of the ballroom?" Grace asked, dropping onto the edge of Hope's bed.

"He made a beeline for Lord Draughton and the two of them left shortly after that." Heavens! Hope touched a hand to her heart. "You don't think he'll tell Lord Draughton about the coaching accident, do you?"

Grace scrunched up her nose. "I don't know to what benefit. Why would Draughton even care? It's not as though he's a friend of Mama's."

That was true. Perhaps Lord Kilworth talking to Lord Draughton had nothing to do with Hope. But what if it did? What if he intended to tell *everyone* about the accident? He'd probably wait until after their negotiations failed, right? "He's going to come here tomorrow." She collapsed against her pillows in defeat.

"Do you think he means to tell Mama himself?"

Drat! Would he do that? "He said we could negotiate further in the park."

"He'll wait to talk to you first, then. " Grace blew out a

breath. "So you'll just have to convince him not to say anything during your ride."

There was the devil's chance of that working. Hope was always more likely to be the one talked *into* things rather than being the one doing the talking. Of the three of them, Grace was the best negotiator. If only—"I've got it!" She sat back up and grinned at her sister. "*You* can go instead of me."

"I beg your pardon?" Grace's voice raised an octave.

But it was the most perfect idea. Hope reached for her sister's hand. "He doesn't know us well enough to tell us apart. He already thought you were me once."

Grace's brow furrowed. "And what am I supposed to say to him?"

"Just convince him to keep his mouth closed. You're so much better at this sort of thing than I am. A ride in the carriage with *you* and he'll never even think to talk to me again."

"That doesn't sound terribly complimentary."

Perhaps not, but it was the truth. When in the proper mood, no one in the world had a sharper tongue than Grace. "Just pretend he's Lord Prestwood and put him firmly in his place. Scare him so soundly that he'll never think to cross you…er…*me* in the future."

Grace heaved a sigh. "In the first place, no one in the world is as inept as Prestwood."

Lord Prestwood was perfectly fine, even if Grace did hate the very sight of the man. "Please?" Hope begged.

Her sister scrubbed a hand down her face. "I hardly think Mr. Lacy would approve if he found out."

Was that all? "Who's going to tell him?" Hope asked, grinning from ear to ear. "Besides, if Lord Kilworth hadn't been such a black-hearted beast that night at the theatre, you might *still* be waiting for Mr. Lacy to propose."

One of Grace's eyebrows lifted. "When put that way, I should be doing *him* a favor and not you."

Hope rolled her eyes. As though Grace would ever side with Lord Kilworth over her own sister. "You will do it, won't you? Help me untangle this mess I've somehow gotten myself into?"

"I'll do it," Grace breathed out. "But you have to tell me everything, every single thing the two of you have said to each other, or I'll never pull it off."

There wasn't that much to tell. In fact, Hope was fairly certain she had already told Grace every bit of it, but her sister was doing her a favor. So Hope started again from the beginning. "Jamie and I were chasing after Alice Humphreys' barouche…"

∼

The Posts' white parlor was *very* white, not even a hint of any other color as Thad glanced around the room for the hundredth time. He'd been waiting ten minutes already and wondered exactly how long Lady Hope intended to make him cool his heels. He'd spent the entire morning and the better part of the previous night thinking about her. The missing sparkle in her eyes, the plumpness of her bottom lip, the creamy swells hinted at beneath her bodice. And she had the most intoxicating scent, like wisteria on a breezy spring day, the memory of which had kept him awake for several hours. It was all slightly maddening.

"Lord Kilworth?" Her lyrical voice from the threshold made Thad's breath catch in his throat.

He spun on his heels and couldn't help but smile. She was beautiful, strikingly so. "My lady, you do look lovely." And she did, but there was something unusual about her that morning. Lady Hope held herself more proudly than she had last night, and her eyes…Well, they were still missing their sparkle, but there was something else that didn't seem quite right, not that he knew her very well at all.

She heaved an irritated sigh. "A ride in the park, wasn't it? Let's do get this over with."

So no banter today. That was unfortunate. She'd been so charming last night. "Are you feeling all right?"

She narrowed her eyes on him and a chill rippled through Thad. "How unusual for a blackmailer to care one way or the other."

Oh, for God's sake. He wasn't really blackmailing her. Besides, hadn't they decided that they were *negotiating*? It was all just flirtation in any event. "Well…" he began.

But an older lady with blonde and silver hair appeared in the doorway at that moment, "Grace!" she snapped. "I thought you were going to do something about *that girl*."

Grace? She was *Lady Grace*! Why the devil was Grace Post passing herself off as her sister? A muscle began to twitch in Thad's jaw. Did the two of them think they could play him for a fool? They likely would have if their mother hadn't spoiled their plans. But to what end?

Lady Grace's face turned slightly red. "Mama, can't we discuss this later?"

"We will discuss it now," her mother said, and apparently didn't realize Thad was in the parlor. "That girl is wholly unacceptable, and you are well aware of the fact. You were supposed to talk to Mr. Lacy—"

Lady Grace sucked in a breath. "Hope has company, Mama." And she tipped her head towards Thad.

The dowager Marchioness of Bradenham glanced from her daughter to Thad and a bit of color stained her cheeks. "I'm terribly sorry. I didn't realize."

"I'm Kilworth," Thad introduced himself.

And the bit of color on the marchioness' face went from a

slight pink to a blood red in half a second. "Kilworth?" she nearly shrieked.

From her reaction, it was quite clear that the marchioness had not been terribly fond of Thad's predecessor. Something the two of them had in common. "I assure you, Lady Bradenham, I am not cut from the same cloth as my late-cousin."

Lady Grace snorted which pulled her mother's attention back to her. "Go get your sister, Grace. Then we will continue *our* conversation in just a moment."

~

Blast it! Hope knew she shouldn't nibble on her nails, but she was just so nervous, she couldn't help it. Hopefully, Grace could pull off a miracle where Lord Kilworth was concerned, but… she glanced down at the jagged edges of her nails and winced. Heavens, her fingers looked atrocious. She'd be wearing gloves to bed for the next fort—

The door to her chambers burst open and Grace stumbled inside, her face flushed and looking positively panicked.

"Good heavens!" Hope's hand fluttered to her heart. Her sister couldn't have dispensed with Lord Kilworth so quickly, could she? Had he done something awful to put Grace in such a state? "What happened?"

"Mama," Grace whispered. "She came upon us. She said *my* name. He knows I'm me and he's waiting for you."

Hope's stomach twisted and she was fairly certain she was going to be ill. "He's waiting for me?" What in the world was she going to say to the blackguard?

"Mama is *still* with him," her sister added urgently.

Drat it all! What if he was telling Mama right at that moment that Hope had been the one driving Jamie's phaeton in the park the other day? Without another word for her sister, Hope brushed past Grace and raced as quickly as she was able in her slippers to the white parlor.

"I'm certain you can understand my trepidation." Mama's voice drifted down the corridor and Hope slowed her gait so she could hear the conversation better.

"Considering my cousin's reputation, Lady Bradenham," came Kilworth's voice, "your worries are completely understandable. But I can assure you, my highest priority as earl is to return the Kilworth name to its formerly untarnished prestige."

Formerly untarnished prestige. Hope couldn't help but frown. Henry was dead. Must everyone, even his own flesh, continue to speak ill of him?

"Happy as I am to hear that, I'm certain you can appreciate that any attention you bestow upon Hope will only remind the *ton* further of her association with your predecessor. That would be most unfortunate for my daughter."

Heaven forbid anyone remember Henry fondly. Hope's blood began to boil.

"It was complete happenstance that she bumped into me in the park—"

Heavens! He couldn't finish that sentence.

Hope burst into the parlor, her heart pounding in her chest. "We're to go for a ride, weren't we, Lord Kilworth?"

He pushed off the settee at her entrance, and his dark gaze settled on her. Hope's breath caught in her throat. Blast him for having any sort of effect on her at all. And blast him for being so singularly handsome.

CHAPTER 5

*A*h, yes. *That* blonde, with her flushed cheeks and panicked emerald eyes, standing just inside the parlor was most definitely Lady Hope. At least Thad thought she was. The girl *did* have another identical sister. But they wouldn't try to pull the wool over his eyes a second time, would they? Not with their mother right there in the parlor with him? "As long as we have Lady Bradenham's blessing." And once he had that blessing, he and Lady Hope were going to have a very long conversation about this most recent deceit.

The dowager marchioness looked from Thad to Lady Hope, her brow furrowed. "I suppose I *could* chaperone the two of you."

Well, that was counterproductive to his purposes. "I'm afraid there's only room for two in Cole's phaeton." Which was the main point in possessing such a conveyance. Well, that and the thrill of racing, of course.

"I beg your pardon?" Lady Bradenham's brow furrowed even further in confusion.

What did she not understand? He chanced a glance

toward Lady Hope whose cheeks were still a rather endearing pink. "Cole's phaeton only has room for two," he said again, slightly differently, thinking perhaps word order might explain away whatever it was her ladyship had not understood.

"You thought to take my daughter for a ride in the park in a *borrowed* phaeton?" She sounded on the edge of histrionics, to be honest. She was tightly wound, wasn't she?

"Mama," Lady Hope whispered.

"Do you not have your own conveyance, Lord Kilworth?" Lady Bradenham speared him with a horrified expression.

Honestly, what business was it of hers whether he owned a conveyance or not? The truth was, he owned a number of them, but a nice phaeton only had room for two and his was currently in Mr. Davies's shop. "Well, I—"

"Mama!" Lady Hope nearly squealed. "Lord Kilworth has a perfectly nice phaeton, but Jamie crashed into him. Remember?" And she shot Thad a murderous expression as though daring him to contradict her.

Ah! That's what this was about. Lady Bradenham would lose her mind if she knew her daughter had been *driving* that day in the park. And that was why she thought Thad meant to blackmail her. Well, that was interesting, wasn't it? He couldn't help but smile in return.

"Indeed," he agreed, thoroughly enjoying himself as he let his gaze settle on the blonde he'd thought so much about the last few days. "Lord Robert offered me the use of his phaeton while mine is in the process of repair."

"Oh!" Lady Bradenham's hand fluttered to her chest. "I hadn't realized the incident Hope and James were involved in had caused any sort of damage. Was anyone hurt?"

"We were fortunate not to have suffered injury to any humans or equines in the collision."

"I don't know what was wrong with my nephew that day. It's quite unlike him to behave so recklessly."

But not so unlike her daughter just a few feet away. Reckless Lady Hope who had first captured Thad's notice with that infamous romp through the Serpentine the previous year. "Perhaps he's easily influenced, my lady," Thad replied, which earned him a scathing look from Lady Hope. It was quite impossible for her to be any lovelier than she was right then, color in her cheeks, her emerald eyes flashing indignantly, and all the while trying to appear composed in front of her mother. Thad wasn't certain when he'd had so much fun. "Or distracted," he tossed in for good measure. Lady Hope could, after all, probably distract a saint.

"He was quite intent on catching Miss Humphreys' barouche that afternoon," the tempting blonde added.

Her mother frowned at that. Then she turned her attention back on Thad. "You won't have her gone too long, will you, my lord?"

Only as long as he was able. Thad shook his head. "Just a quick ride through the park, Lady Bradenham, though I suppose we could always encounter an acquaintance or two along the way."

The dowager marchioness acknowledged that with a nod of her head. "Very well."

Thad started towards the threshold and offered his arm to Lady Hope. He managed to hide his grin as she begrudgingly slid her dainty hand around the crook of his arm.

~

Awful, irritating, manipulative jackanapes! If Hope never saw Lord Kilworth again, it would be too soon.

"Aren't you a cunning little minx?" he asked as he led her through the front door and out onto the stoop.

That was hardly complimentary. Hope glared up at the earl. "Still as charming as ever, I see."

A shadow of a smile graced his face as though he was truly enjoying himself. Despicable blackguard. "Did you truly think it would be so easy to fool me?" he asked, guiding her to his borrowed phaeton. Then he placed both hands on her waist and lifted her up into the conveyance. Heavens! The heat from his touch nearly seared her.

Hope gasped at his familiarity. "I can manage on my own," she grumbled. Why in the world would a touch from him make her feel…anything?

And that smile of his grew even wider like he knew he'd affected her somehow. Blast him. He rounded the back of the phaeton and then settled beside her on the seat. "I'm sure you won't object if *I* drive. Less dangerous that way, don't you agree?" he said so condescendingly, Hope wanted to slug him.

Less dangerous. She tipped her head back and narrowed her eyes on the earl. "Until I push you over the side to your death."

He laughed as he urged the pair of matched bays forward. "I am not sure how I ever mistook you for your sister, Lady Hope. I can promise that I will never do so again."

He certainly wouldn't be the first to think so, but Hope, Grace and Patience had done a fair amount of impersonating each other over the years. Well…Hope and Grace had done so. Patience couldn't keep a secret if her life depended upon it. "As I have no plans to see you in the future, Lord Kilworth, I suppose we'll never know the truth one way or the other."

"You do wound me," he said, sounding fairly far from wounded as his horses continued onto South Street. "And I thought we had such a delightful time sparring with each other."

Spending time with *him* was not delightful in the least. But Hope bit her tongue from saying as much to keep from sparring with the man, since he seemed to enjoy it so much. Thankfully, they continued in silence for a bit, at least until they approached Park Lane.

"You aren't quite the same as I remember you from last year, however," Lord Kilworth said softly.

Last year? On her life, Hope had never encountered the man until a few days ago. She glanced up at him only to find the earl's eyes firmly on the road before them. "We've *never* met before," she said. And they hadn't. She would have remembered his arrogance had their paths ever crossed.

"In the park," he said evenly. "You were romping through the Serpentine with my cousin. It's a memory I'll never forget."

He had been in the park *that day?* Heavens. She'd never live that day down as long as she lived. Henry had snatched the strand of pearls from around her neck. He *had* possessed the cleverest of fingers. It was foolish of Hope to follow him into the Serpentine trying to get the necklace back. Looking back on that, she'd been so idiotic. But in the heat of the moment, and worried her mother would kill her if something happened to the heirloom, she'd followed Henry right into the water. He'd looked so surprised when she'd splashed into the water after him. And then he'd smiled so purely, so honestly, if she hadn't already been in love with him, she'd have fallen that day.

She'd slipped in the water and ended up bringing Henry right down with her. They'd both been drenched from head to toe. She could even remember the horrid taste of that water in her mouth. But nothing else had mattered, nothing other than Henry. "It was not one of my better days," she said, missing the loss of Henry all over again. She could live to be 500, and she'd never get over losing him.

"Yes, well, you certainly made an impression," he said as they turned onto Park Lane and headed toward the Park. "I'm not sure if I ever saw a more beautiful sight in my life." That last part he said so softly she wasn't certain if he'd even said it at all. And she wasn't certain if she wanted to hear him. What was she supposed to say to that?

"Perhaps it wasn't even me that day. Perhaps it was one of my sisters pretending to be me," she said, wishing she wasn't suddenly so aware of how close his leg was to hers on the bench. Heavens, what was wrong with her?

"I don't know the first thing about your sister who's married to the doctor in Yorkshire, but there is no way in the world the girl splashing in the Serpentine was Lady Grace."

"And how are you so certain?"

That smile of his was back in place again. "She doesn't live life the same way you do. There's this passion, adventure right beneath your skin just waiting to come out. Your sister could give a man frostbite with just a glance."

And Grace might very well take a dueling pistol to Lord Kilworth if she heard him say such a thing about her. "Grace has confidence," Hope returned.

"And *you* have spirit," he said evenly, casting her a sidelong glance. "But you used to have a sparkle in your eyes, though I haven't seen evidence of it this season."

A sparkle in her eyes. Henry used to say the same thing about her eyes. "I'm not certain it will ever return," she said, nodding to Lord and Lady Wolverly in a gig along Rotten Row.

"Why not?" he asked, and seemed like he genuinely cared about the answer.

Hope shrugged and looked out at the sea of fashionable people crowding the park. "I lost the love of my life, Lord

Kilworth. I've felt like a stranger in my own skin for months." And she had no idea why she told him that, but he *had* asked; and Henry *had* been his cousin. And perhaps saying as much would keep her from noticing his leg pressed against hers. After all, she didn't even like the man.

"Ah!" Boomed a voice Hope could have gone forever without hearing. "Thaddeus Baxter! How are you, my boy?" Her great-uncle, the intimidating Duke of Danby sat amongst a bevy of beautiful ladies in a large open air landau. His granddaughters. Most of them, it seemed.

Had Danby just called Lord Kilworth by his Christian name? There was something unnerving about that.

"Your Grace," Lord Kilworth returned. "Happy, as always, to see you." He flashed that smile of his at the landau and tipped his bowler hat. "Lady Heathfield, Lady Isabel, Mrs. Trent, Lady Marston, Lady Morley."

The duke's blue eyes landed on Hope and they narrowed slightly. "So which one *are* you?"

"Grandpapa," Lady Heathfield chastised under her breath.

Danby's gaze flashed briefly to the auburn-haired girl as though to silence her before turning his attention back to Hope. "Never mind. You're Hope, aren't you?"

She hadn't even uttered a word. How in the world could he tell which triplet she was? Very few people outside of family could tell her apart from her sisters, and she'd never spent very much time in His Grace's presence. Only a tiny bit this last Christmas, to be honest. "How did you know?"

"Grace would've already snapped at me." And, of course, Patience was in Yorkshire not far from the duke's castle. Danby turned his attention to Lord Kilworth. "How is Margaret faring?"

"She suffered from ague most of the winter, but Mother says she's doing better now that it's warmer."

Margaret? Margaret Baxter, Henry's old maiden aunt?

How well did Danby know the Baxters? Hope swallowed nervously, which was odd. Grace was the one intent on finding a husband before the duke could appoint one for her. Hope hadn't cared one whit. It didn't matter who, if anyone, the duke selected for her. She'd never love again, so what did it matter who he picked out for her? But now…Well, there was something about the fact that Danby seemed so familiar with Lord Kilworth that struck a bit of fear in Hope's heart.

"Do send her my best," Danby said. "And if the doctor in Lealholm is too inept to cure her ague, she is always welcome at Danby Castle. I do believe I have the best doctor in all of Britain."

"Thank you." Lord Kilworth nodded. "I will tell her, Your Grace."

CHAPTER 6

Thad had nodded in farewell to the duke and his granddaughters and then urged his bays forwards once more. His mind was still reeling, however. Lady Hope's words still echoing in his ears. *I lost the love of my life, Lord Kilworth. I've felt like a stranger in my own skin for months.* Had she truly thought herself in love with Henry? Thad knew she'd fancied his cousin. And Henry could be the most charming of men when he wanted to be, but...To actually *love* him?

There was no doubt in Thad's mind that whatever love Lady Hope had felt for his blackguard of a cousin, Henry was both undeserving and did not return her affections. If he had, the two would have been married immediately following the Serpentine incident. But Henry, ever the cad, had not cared one whit about the whispers swirling around Lady Hope ever since that infamous day. A decent man would have married her then, even if he didn't return the lady's affection. But no one had ever mistaken Henry Baxter for a decent man. No one except, perhaps, Lady Hope.

"I had no idea you were so well acquainted with my great-uncle," she said, breaking into Thad's thoughts.

"My great-aunt is an old friend of Danby's late-wife." In fact, he'd known the man most of his life. No one equaled Danby's standing in northern Yorkshire.

"He was much more pleasant to you than he has been with any of us."

Danby had a certain reputation, but he was a decent fellow. Thad couldn't help but smile. "Are you intimidated by His Grace? *You*, the girl who threatened to push me to my death a little while ago?"

Lady Hope shrugged slightly. "We spent Christmas at Danby Castle, and I can assure you the man is singularly focused when he is of a mind." She gestured in the direction Danby's landau had gone. "From what I've heard, he has a stack of special licenses just waiting for his Machiavellian plans to fall into place, seeing each and every unmarried relative settled before his death."

Thad had heard those rumors too, but he imagined Danby had better things to do than play matchmaker at every turn. Odds were His Grace simply let his reputation speak for himself, and his panicked relatives did the rest. "You don't think he has any ducal duties that require his attention?"

"He had a hand in each of his granddaughters' marriages. And this last Christmas, he even secured a match for my sister Patience."

Thad tipped his hat at Lord and Lady Berkswell walking along the row, then he cast a sidelong glance at Lady Hope again. "Is that why he intimidates you? You're concerned about him matchmaking on your behalf?"

A sad smile settled on her face. "Grace and Jamie have been on matrimony missions all Season long they've been so worried about him."

James Woodward was scared, was he? There was something amusing about that. Of course, with Lady Grace's icy demeanor, *she* had every right to be worried about such an occurrence. What kind of fellow would Danby dig up that could tolerate her for a life time? Probably only Daniel Lacy would willingly subject himself to her scintillating personality. Not that Thad cared about Lady Hope's sister in the least. Of course, the enchanting blonde sitting next to him on the bench was another matter all together. "What about you, my lady? Have you been worried as well?"

"Not in the least."

Smart girl. She had no reason to be concerned. Lovely and enchanting as Lady Hope was, some fellow would snatch her up before the Season came to a close, Thad had no doubt. "I imagine you have nothing to worry about. Though any fellow who *does* offer for you should be warned not to let you drive any of his conveyances."

"You are the worst sort of villain, my lord."

"I'm certain my sister would agree with you wholeheartedly," he laughed.

"Oh? Were you a terrible brother?"

Years ago Sarah would have said yes to that without hesitation. "We get along perfectly well these days." Even if Thad didn't particularly care for his brother-in-law.

"*These* days?" she echoed. "Is that a new development, then? Did you take to blackmailing her in your youth?"

"I believe the word you're looking for is *negotiating*, my lady."

She laughed and he couldn't help smiling. She really did have the most delightful laugh, warm and honest. Who was courting her? Why wasn't she afraid of her great-uncle's stack of special licenses?

He cast her a sidelong glance. "Should I be worried someone will call me out over our negotiations?"

She frowned slightly at that. "Fairly certain my brothers would strangle me for driving Jamie's phaeton before they called you out. So I'd rather they not ever learn the truth."

Just her brothers? "I shan't breathe a word to either of them," he vowed. "Any suitors I should concern myself with? I'd hate to be caught unaware."

"The only suitor who would avenge my honor died last autumn."

Henry? When he was alive he'd never avenged anyone's honor, and Thad highly doubted his cousin would do so now if he was still alive. But was there really no one else? "And yet the threat of Danby's special licenses doesn't concern you?"

She shrugged. "Whether he has one with my name or not makes no difference at all," she replied softly. "With Henry gone, my future is meaningless. So why would it matter if His Grace has a match for me or not?"

Was she serious? Thad shifted on the bench to see her better. Lady Hope was young, vivacious, stunning, engaging, and the most enchanting girl he'd ever encountered. She couldn't really mean to throw the rest of her life away because his blackguard of a cousin was dead. She had so much to live for, so much to look forward to.

But according to the lady, Henry's death was the sole reason for a lack of sparkle in her eyes these days. What if Thad could give that back to her? He could at least try, couldn't he? It was the least he could do after his cousin nearly ruined her. "There is nothing meaningless about you, Lady Hope, let alone your future."

∼

Hope glanced up to find Lord Kilworth's dark blue eyes focused on her. The sincerity in his depths made her breath catch in her throat. "You don't have to say that."

"I don't have to say anything," he agreed. "And, yet, I can't seem to help myself. I hardly doubt my cousin was worthy of your devotion."

Hope released a sigh. "He was your cousin. Can you not find something nice to say about him? No one seems able, and it's made me feel even more isolated from the world. I can't be the only one to have seen the true nature of him."

The look on Lord Kilworth's face was fairly dismissive of that. "I knew Henry my entire life, Lady Hope, don't you think it's possible that if one of the two of us knew his true nature, it would be me?"

Hope refused to acknowledge that he might be correct, because she had known Henry too. She knew a side of him no one else had, apparently. And she still loved him. She would until the end of her days. "I know he was a bit of a rogue, but there was much more to him than that."

"You are too generous." Lord Kilworth blew out a breath and directed his bays towards the far end of the park.

Once they had gone far enough that no one was nearby, he pulled back on the reins, drew the phaeton to a stop, and looped the ribbons around the hook. Then he turned on the bench, his knee pressing against Hope's leg, which made awareness shoot through her. What *was* it about him?

"On my word," he began, his gaze searing her once more. "You are the most enchanting girl I've ever encountered. And I'll be damned if you'll toss the rest of your life away because *he's* gone."

Hope swallowed nervously. What was she to say to that? "I hardly see why it's any of your concern."

And then he cupped her face with his hands, his dark eyes staring so intently into hers that she felt it deep in her core. "And yet I'm concerned all the same," he said softly as he leaned forwards...

Heavens, he meant to kiss her! What if it was a horrible

kiss like Jamie shared with Alice Humphreys? What if it ruined the memory she had of Henry's kiss. What if…

Lord Kilworth's warm lips pressed to hers and heat shot through Hope. Her eyes fluttered closed and she grasped the edge of his jacket, breathing in the citric cent of his shaving lotion and she couldn't quite think about anything else. He moaned slightly against her lips and the sensation reverberated through her.

Heavens! It wasn't a horrible kiss. It was a wonderful kiss, heady and intoxicating. A tingle raced along Hope's skin and she couldn't help but lean into him.

And then Lord Kilworth lifted his head and Hope's eyes popped open. Oh, good heavens, what had she done? He brushed a finger across her cheek before releasing her. " What are your plans this evening?"

Plans? Did she have plans? Her mind was a jumble. How was she supposed to remember anything with him looking at her so intently? "Um, the St. Austell soiree."

He smiled then. "Save me a waltz?"

That sounded like such a terrible idea. Reckless and dangerous. He'd already kissed her, and…Well, she didn't really even like him. Or did she? She *had* liked his kiss. What did that say about her? Nothing good, certainly. But Hope nodded anyway. She couldn't quite help herself.

Lord Kilworth said very little as he drove her back to Post House, and Hope was thankful for the reprieve. She had no idea what she thought about anything that had happened that afternoon and needed to clear her head. That was still difficult to do with him so close to her on the bench, however. His thigh was pressed against hers and the heat from him seeped through the muslin of her dress and warmed every inch of her.

He stopped his borrowed phaeton in front of Post House and looped the reins around the hook. Then he hopped down and navigated his way around the back of the conveyance, stopping right next to Hope.

"Allow me?" he asked, reaching his hands out to her.

Heavens. To have his hands on her again…

He grasped her waist and easily plucked her from the bench and gently placed her back on her feet before him.

Hope stared up at him, swallowing a bit nervously.

"The St. Austell soiree?" he asked, his voice rumbling over her.

And she nodded, just as the front door opened and Mama and Aunt Rachel stepped out onto the front stoop.

"Oh!" Mama said and scowled slightly at Lord Kilworth. "Wonderful, you're back already. Your aunt and I were just about to go for a stroll. You can join us."

Hope blew out a breath. The last thing she wanted to do was go for a walk with her mother and aunt. She'd never get her thoughts in order if she was with the two of them. "I'd promised Grace and Lila we'd go shopping, Mama," she lied, praying her sister and sister-in-law were still home.

Her mother cast one more scathing glance in Lord Kilworth's direction. "Then we'll talk when you return."

Hope smiled up at the earl and said, "Thank you so much for the ride, my lord," before brushing past her mother and aunt up the steps and into the house.

CHAPTER 7

⁂

*A*s soon as Hope stepped over the threshold, she heard Vivaldi flowing from the music room. Grace must be in a mood, but there was no one else Hope could confide in. So her sister would just have to get out of whatever mood she was in.

She made a direct path to the music room, and Grace was poised on the bench with her eyes closed while her fingers flew over the keys. Hope stood in the doorway a moment, listening to the music as her thoughts returned to that sudden kiss in the park. Never in her wildest imagination would she have ever thought Lord Kilworth would kiss her, not the current Lord Kilworth in any event. But he had and it still made her breathless to remember.

She must have made some sort of sound because Grace sucked in a breath and spun around on the bench. "Honestly!" She touched a hand to her heart. "You took ten years off my life."

"Sorry," Hope muttered, stepping further into the room and dropping onto a divan against the wall. "I didn't want to disturb you."

"I didn't mean to snap." Grace pinched the bridge over her nose. "Mama is just pushing me to the limits of my patience."

Which explained Vivaldi and Grace's mood. "Why? What is she doing now?"

Grace shook her head in annoyance. "She's being unbearable about Daniel's sister and it's putting me in an awful spot with him."

Mr. Lacy's bastard sister. Yes, Mama had been rather put out about the whole thing. "I am sorry." Hope frowned.

"He adores his sister. He wants her at the wedding and he is entitled to have his sister there." Grace slid off the bench and started towards Hope's divan. "It was hard enough bringing him up to scratch in the first place. Why does she have to make the whole thing more difficult?"

Hope heaved a sigh as her sister dropped into the space beside her. "Any whisper of scandal or impropriety and she's unwavering to the nth degree." They all knew that. Mama had been that way their entire lives. It was nearly suffocating being her daughter. "You should have seen the way she glared at Lord Kilworth just now."

"Maybe that will help you scare him away," Grace said, tilting her head as though to see Hope better. "I am sorry I wasn't able to do so before she stumbled upon us."

If Grace had gone to the park with Lord Kilworth, would he have tried to kiss her instead? She hoped not, which was a foolish thing to hope for. "I'm not certain I want to scare him away," she said softly.

Her sister looked at her as though she'd sprouted a second nose. "The man is blackmailing you."

But she didn't think he was. In fact, she thought she'd misjudged that whole situation entirely. "He kissed me," Hope said quickly and looked away from her sister's perceptive eyes.

"I beg your pardon?" Grace whispered.

Still Hope couldn't look at her. "It was different than Henry, but it was—" she sighed "—completely breathtaking."

"Why in the world would you kiss *that* man?" Grace breathed out in apparent shock. "He called you a menace, let me remind you."

He had done that, and Hope hadn't really forgiven him for that. But she didn't really think he was the villain she'd originally thought either. Not with the concern in his eyes, not with the gentleness in his touch. "I didn't plan on it," she protested. "But he did kiss me and he asked me to save him a waltz tonight and…"

"Once again, you have lost your mind." Grace heaved a sigh. "I think you should make a vow to never even *speak* to a man named Kilworth for the rest of your days, let alone kiss one."

Hope finally glanced over at her sister. "He's as fond of Henry as you are."

Grace's green eyes widened a little in surprise at that. "I suppose that does say *something* for his character, then."

Hope smacked her sister's leg. "You're not supposed to speak ill of the dead."

"I said worse when he was alive," Grace grumbled. Then she shook her head. "You don't actually like him, do you? The new Lord Kilworth, I mean. I know how you felt about the late one."

Hope shrugged slightly. "I'm not sure what I think. I think I like him a little. I did like his kiss, which surprised me. I never thought I'd like any kiss again for the rest of my life. And after Jamie—"

"For heaven's sake!" Grace gasped. "You didn't kiss *Jamie*!"

Kiss Jamie? What—? "No!" Hope shook her head. Why in the world would Grace think *that*? "That would be like kissing Quent or Braden?" What a completely nauseating thought.

Her sister looked slightly relieved. "Then what did you mean by 'And after Jamie'?"

Oh good heavens! "If you'd let me finish my sentence, Grace Post!" Hope glared slightly at her sister. "After Jamie told me about his awful kiss, I didn't think I'd ever experience a good kiss for the rest of my life."

"Jamie had an awful kiss?" Grace echoed.

"Alice Humphreys. But neither of us are supposed to know that, so don't breathe a word of it to anyone."

Grace's lips pursed like she'd been forced to eat a lemon. "I would hardly think *she* could muster up enough passion to kiss decently in the first place. What awful taste our cousin has."

"Has Mr. Lacy kissed you?" Hope asked, though she rarely broached anything of a personal nature with Grace. They were just so different and Grace was so private.

Her sister looked uncomfortable all of a sudden. "Of course."

"And was it a good kiss or a bad kiss?"

Grace shook her head. "It was perfectly pleasant."

Perfectly pleasant sounded perfectly awful. "Pleasant?" Hope shook her head. "Do you want to spend the rest of your life with a man who is just perfectly pleasant? Don't you want your heart to soar and for passion to pound through your veins and—"

"I'm certain you've experienced enough passion for both of us," Grace replied, sounding slightly clipped. "And Mr. Lacy is exactly want I want, Hope. He is kind and pleasant. Intelligent, honorable. What more could I want in a husband?"

Perhaps more than just perfectly pleasant. Perhaps just a taste of the adventure and passion Hope experienced with

Henry, and perhaps…She shook her head. She really shouldn't think about the new Lord Kilworth in the same way, even if his kiss *had* left her breathless.

"Did you say Lord Kilworth wanted you to save him a waltz tonight?"

Hope couldn't help but smile at the thought of the dashing earl holding her in his arms. "Mmm."

Her sister giggled. "Then you'll look quite ridiculous being the only pair waltzing during the Hayward musicale."

The Hayward musicale? "We have the St. Austell soiree tonight."

But Grace shook her head. "We have the St. Austell soiree *tomorrow* night."

Panic seized Hope's heart. She'd told him the wrong event. Her mind had been so jumbled from his kiss, she was lucky she even knew her own name at the time. But she'd told him the wrong event for the evening, and there was no way to tell him of her error. It wasn't as though she could send a note to Baxter House. Not one of her brother's footmen would deliver such a missive to a bachelor residence.

"Drat!"

CHAPTER 8

*W*ell, there was nothing quite like making a fool of one's self, like showing up at the St. Austell's for a soiree that wasn't occurring. Thad felt like an idiot. Had she done that on purpose? He thought there was a very good chance she had. After all, Lady Hope *had* tried to switch places with her sister so she wouldn't have to see him that afternoon. But…Well, she hadn't been indifferent to his kiss. He knew that, and he'd thought she liked him some by the end of their ride in the park.

So why would she purposely make a fool out of him? Was she just perverse? She *had* involved herself with Henry. So that was a possibility.

Thad wasn't quite sure what to think about the whole thing as he strode through he doors at Whites and handed his coat to the footman.

He spotted Robert Cole in the club, chatting with Albert Potsdon, and made a direct path for his friend. He gestured to a passing footman for a whisky and then dropped into one of the chairs across from Robert.

"Thought you were off to the St. Austell soiree," Robert said, leaning back in his chair.

"That's tomorrow," Postsdon chimed in, though no one had asked him.

"Tomorrow?" Thad asked. "Are you certain?"

Potsdon nodded. "Lady St. Austell handed me the invitation herself. Old friend of the family."

Huh. So was Hope Post scatterbrained or perverse? That was the question, wasn't it? "Must've had my days mixed up," Thad replied, though he felt Robert's eyes on him and didn't appreciate the scrutiny.

Luckily, the footman brought Thad his glass of whisky at that moment and he didn't have to meet his friend's gaze. Damn it all, he really shouldn't have landed on the St. Austell's front step on the wrong day and without having been invited. "Do you think you could secure me an invitation to her soiree tomorrow night?" He was an old friend of the family, after all.

Potsdon shrugged. "Consider it done."

One less thing to worry about, then.

"Potsdon said you should speak with Berkswell," Robert said after a moment.

"Oh, indeed!" Albert Potsdon's eyes lit up. "Building new churches sounds like just the thing he'd support."

Thad had already spoken with Berkswell and had the man's support, but as Postdon was helping him get an invite to the St. Austells', he simply nodded in response. "Thank you for the recommendation."

"Of course, of course." The portly man smiled. "If you'll excuse me a moment." He pushed out of his seat and started towards a small group of men not too far away.

Robert waited just long enough for Potsdon to be out of earshot before he asked, "Is she leading you on a wild goose chase?"

"I'm not sure." There was no need to clarify who she was, not with Robert. "But if I catch her, I'm not sure that I'll care."

Robert's eyes widened slightly at that. "And what will you do *if* you catch her."

"I'm not sure that I know that either." Though he'd definitely like to enjoy taking his time catching her, sparring with her, kissing her as often as he was able. *If* he had the time. He might not. He took a sip of his whisky and then asked, "Do you think there's any truth to the rumors about the Duke of Danby?"

"You'll have to be more specific than that." His friend laughed.

"Point taken," Thad conceded as he heaved a sigh. "You've heard the rumors that Danby has dabbled in matchmaking, that he keeps a stack of special licenses, haven't you?"

Robert nodded. "It doesn't sound logical though. Doesn't His Grace have better things to do?"

That was exactly what Thad thought too. But he probably should make certain. What if Danby already had a husband all picked out for Hope? Whoever the fellow was, he wouldn't appreciate Thad sparring with or kissing his wife-to-be. "I should probably make certain in any event."

"Sounds like the fastest way to get a bullseye on your back," Robert remarked before taking a sip of his own drink.

But Thad knew Danby. He'd known him all his life. There was nothing to worry about from the duke. He wasn't nearly as frightening as his reputation would suggest.

∾

Upon his arrival at Whitton House, Thad was shown directly into Danby's study. The old duke greeted him with a nod of his head. "Thaddeus, what a surprise. Do come in, do come in." He gestured to one of the seats across his mahogany desk.

"Thank you, Your Grace," he replied, settling into one of the matching chairs. "I hope I'm not interrupting."

Danby gestured dismissively at his desk. "It can all wait. More important things in life, don't you agree?"

"Like the building of new churches." Thad agreed with an incline of his head.

"Bah." The duke shrugged. "Do you know I spent this morning bouncing one great-grandson on my knee while reading a story to a whole gaggle of my other great-grandchildren? Nothing is more important than that."

Perhaps not to Danby, but England was still in desperate need of more churches. "Did you know in St. Marylebone there are seats enough for 8,000 bodies at church, but over 76,000 people? With the shift in population, sir—"

"Tell me you didn't really seek me out to talk about *churches*, Thaddeus."

Well, it was part of the reason. It's what he'd spent the majority of the season talking about with powerful and influential peers. But the rest of his visit had something to do with an enchanting blonde he couldn't stop thinking about even if she was leading him on a wild goose chase. "In all honesty, I did hear an interesting piece of *on dit* in regards to you, Your Grace."

"From that blonde you were in the park with yesterday?" Danby's blue eyes twinkled just a bit. "Tell me, what does my great-niece say?"

Damn the man for being too observant by half. Thad tugged slightly at his cravat. "Do you really have a stack of special licenses in your possession?"

A ghost of a smile tipped the edges of the duke's lips. "She told you that, did she?"

Did that mean Danby did or did not have a stack of

special licenses? "She said your great-nieces and nephews are falling all over themselves trying to secure matches before you make some sort of decree in regards to them."

At that, the old man sat back in his chair and chuckled. "I should come to Town more often. I've had quite a lively time this season."

Thad had never considered Danby maddening until now. Why was the duke being so evasive? "I am glad to hear it, sir, but…"

"Does Hope want to know if I've secured a match for her? Did she make you her errand boy?"

Hardly that. Thad snorted. "She doesn't seem to care one way or the other, but…"

"But…?" Danby encouraged.

Damn it all. Best just to say it, right? "Well, Your Grace, *I* want to know if you've already picked out some fellow for her."

"And what if I have?" The duke folded his arms across his chest.

"Well, sir, I—" Thad cleared his throat. What if Danby had already handpicked someone for Lady Hope? Thad's days of sparring with and kissing the girl would be over. "Well, I've always trusted your judgment, of course, but—"

"I have never known you to beat around the bush, Thaddeus."

"Well, I suppose I feel responsible for Lady Hope."

"Responsible?"

Thad nodded. "My cousin did not give her the respect he should have, and if it wasn't for Henry, she might be in a very different situation now. And if you *do* have some fellow picked out, I just want to make certain that—"

"That's not what you wanted to ask me," Danby interrupted him.

Thad's mouth dropped open. "It's not?"

And an all-knowing look settled on the duke's face. "What do you mean that Hope doesn't care one way or the other if I've picked someone for her?"

Thad released a breath. "She seems resigned to whatever her future holds. She says that with Henry gone, it doesn't matter what happens to her and—"

"What a ridiculous thing to say. She has decades left to live, and your cousin was a degenerate."

Thad's thoughts exactly. "Be that as it may, if your plan was to spur your great-nieces and nephews into action, it has not worked in Lady Hope's case."

"So, then I *should* pick someone for the girl?"

He rather wished the man wouldn't, but Danby did not appear as though he could be reasoned with today. "If the fellow is decent and will care for her, and—"

"Do you think I would pick a fellow who would treat her poorly?" Danby snapped.

Damn it all, the last thing he wanted to do was insult the duke. "No, of course not, Your Grace."

"Perfect, then I have just the man for her."

Thad's stomach tightened. It was none of his concern, not really. So he'd never forget that kiss, so there wasn't anything quite as enjoyable as sparring with Lady Hope, so he'd thought about her almost since the moment she crashed into his phaeton…She wasn't his concern, but he still had to know. "Who?" he breathed out.

The duke smirked. "Well, you, of course. You do seem concerned about the girl. Who better than you?"

Him? The air whooshed from Thad's lungs. "Well, Your Grace, I hardly know the lady, and her mother is not quite enthralled with me, and—"

"Her mother's an idiot. I can handle my niece," Danby grumbled. "Had she guided her daughters properly, Grace wouldn't have the sharpest tongue in England, and Hope wouldn't have involved herself with your cousin." He released a sigh. "Patience is very nicely settled in Danby with my physician, the most docile and level-headed of the three of them, you can take my word for that."

Docile. James Woodward had said Lady Hope was more docile this year. He hoped she wouldn't become more docile than she was now. He rather liked her spirit, actually. In so many ways she was perfect. But he couldn't really contemplate marrying her. Could he? He did enjoy kissing her and he supposed he *could* right the wrong Henry had caused if he married her, but that didn't seem like the best reasons to marry a girl. He'd truly only wanted to make certain that she'd be matched with some decent fellow, if Danby was dead set on securing matches. He hadn't meant to throw his hat into the ring, so to speak. "I'm not certain we'd suit," he finally said.

"Afraid she'll upturn all of your conveyances?" Danby's smirk became a full-fledged smile.

"I beg your pardon?" Thad stammered. How in the world did Danby know about that?

"Do you really think there's anything I don't know or can't find out?" The duke chuckled. "Do think about it, Thaddeus. If I don't put your name on one my special licenses, it'll be some other fellow. And do you really want me to do that? Name some fellow other than you?"

"I simply wanted to make certain she'd be cared for, I—"

"Then who better than you to make certain of that very thing?" the duke countered. "Besides you like the girl. I can tell you do. And she comes from a decent family. You'll need a wife of your own someday. So why not Hope?"

"Well, I barely know her." Even though he would like to know her better. But that wasn't why he'd come today. He hadn't expected any of this. He'd expected Danby would laugh off the idea of special licenses and handpicked fiancés, but that hadn't happened.

"All right." Danby nodded his head. "Then I'll go back to my original choice. No need to worry yourself further about the girl."

His original choice? Who was his original choice? A cold sweat started to seep across Thad. "Your Grace, will you please tell me the fellow's name?"

But the duke shook his head. "Hardly your concern, Thaddeus. And if the man refuses me, I'd rather not cast anymore disparagement on her than your cousin has already done by naming him and having his rejection known."

Damn it all. Thad supposed that made sense, but he felt worse now than he did when he'd first stepped into the duke's study. "Well, then, best of luck to you." And to Hope. The very best of luck to her and whomever Danby thought to match her up with. What if the fellow was horrible? What if he never cared for her and only cared about earning Danby's favor? She deserved better than some sycophantic toady, didn't she?

There was a scratch at the door and the Danby butler cleared his throat. "Your Grace, Lord Heathfield is here to see you."

The duke smiled. "Perfect timing, Kilworth was just leaving." Then he gestured toward the corridor. "I'm certain Heathfield would be happy to support your new churches bill. You should set up a time to see him."

And just that quickly, Thad had been dismissed.

CHAPTER 9

*H*ope glanced across the coach at her brother and his wife. Quent sported a rather knowing grin for some reason. "What are you so happy about?" she asked. After all, she couldn't imagine anyone who'd been summoned to Whitton House that very afternoon would smile about much of anything. Of course, Quent seemed to like the old duke for some reason.

Quent's smile grew like he had some sort of secret. "Just so glad we're not about to attend another dismal musical. And someone—" he winked at his wife Lila "—has said I never have to attend another one."

"You're too kind," Grace grumbled from beside Hope. And she *had* played beautifully the night before. Quent was lucky she hadn't kicked him in the knee after that comment.

But their brother only laughed in response. "You know I love to hear *you*, love. But most of the girls singing were akin to screeching wildcats in a bag."

"Have you much experience with screeching wildcats in bags?" Hope asked as the carriage rambled to a stop in front of a lovely house on Curzon Street. "How does one hold on to such a thing?"

"Carefully, love." Quent nodded. "Very carefully." Then he bounded out of the coach first and offered his hand to Lila. Then he helped Grace and Hope climb from the carriage as well.

Hope linked her arm with her sister's as they climbed the steps to St. Austell House. "Will Mr. Lacy be here this evening?" The man didn't care for dancing, but he had attended a few events this season.

Grace shook her head. "He's in the middle of researching something about infrared radiation, at least I think that's what he said."

Whatever in the world that was. Sometimes Hope wasn't certain if Mr. Lacy was brilliant or just odd. She and her sister crossed into the St. Austell foyer and Hope cast Grace a sidelong glance. "You're certain you want to marry him?" She was fairly certain Mr. Lacy would bore her to death after just a fortnight of marriage. She couldn't imagine spending her lifetime with the man.

"He'll do." Grace heaved a sigh. "Besides there's no telling who our great-uncle would select for me instead. And at least I've chosen Mr. Lacy."

Their great-uncle might have better taste than Grace did, but Hope bit her tongue from saying as much. Not that she disliked Mr. Lacy. The fellow was nice enough, just extraordinarily boring. She couldn't imagine him pretending to blackmail anyone. She couldn't imagine him ever bantering the same way Lord Kilworth did. She couldn't imagine Mr. Lacy's kiss coming anywhere close to Lord Kilworth's. *Perfectly pleasant.* There wasn't anything about Lord Kilworth's kiss that had been perfectly pleasant. Passionate, breath-taking, Earth-shattering were more apt descriptions.

They followed Quent and Lila down the corridor, into the ballroom; and almost as though her earlier musings about the man had conjured him up, Lord Kilworth was near the far wall, conversing with the Prime Minister. When his gaze shifted from Liverpool to fall on Hope, the air whooshed from her lungs and she might have stumbled if her arm wasn't still linked with Grace's.

Her sister snorted. "If I live to be a thousand, I will never understand your taste in men."

Hope quirked a grin in Grace's direction. "And I shall never understand yours, my dear sister."

Lord Kilworth muttered something to the Prime Minister, though his gaze remained focused on Hope, and then he made a direct path towards her.

Hope's belly nearly flipped. He was so dashing and so very handsome, and…

"Ah, Baxter." Quent offered his hand to the earl.

Quent knew Lord Kilworth? She hadn't realized the two of them were acquainted. Of course her brother had been friends with Henry once upon a time. She supposed she shouldn't be surprised by that fact.

"Post." Lord Kilworth accepted Quent's hand and smiled at Lila. "My lady."

"Honestly, a ballroom is the last place I'd ever think to find you," Quent said.

Lord Kilworth's eyes flashed to Hope, making her belly flip all over again. "Yes, well, a certain lady has promised me a waltz, though I may have had the date incorrect."

Hope's cheeks burned slightly. However, she wasn't about to admit her error in front of her family. "I'm afraid they're not playing a waltz, my lord."

"Indeed." The grin he flashed in her direction had the very real possibility of making her melt right in the middle of the ballroom. "Care to take a turn about the room with me while we wait?" He offered her his arm, which she took without hesitation.

Her brother seemed quite amused by the whole thing, which was odd. These days, he rarely noticed anything that wasn't directly related to Lila.

"So did you give me the wrong date for this soiree to make a fool of me, Lady Hope?" Lord Kilworth asked only loud enough for her to hear once they'd left her family behind them.

"I suppose I owe you an apology for that," she returned, not really daring to glance over at him. "But it was your fault."

He laughed at that. "*My* fault?"

She did chance a peek up at him then. "It was impossible to think straight after you kissed me."

A rather pleased expression settled on his face. "Well, then you are quite forgiven." He laughed again. "In fact, that may be the only excuse you could give that I'd find worthy of forgiveness."

He was slightly arrogant, wasn't he? "Yes, well, I probably should never kiss you again, just to keep my mind straight going forward."

"Where would be the fun in that?" Lord Kilworth drew her to a stop and tugged her closer to him.

Hope inhaled the citric of his shaving lotion and managed, just barely, not to sigh.

"I've thought of nothing except kissing you over the last two days." His voice rumbled over her and tingles raced across Hope's skin as his dark blue eyes speared her where she stood.

"Even now, while you were talking to Lord Liverpool?" she asked. "You were thinking of kissing me even then?"

"Even then." He agreed with a wicked twinkle in his eyes. "Sending me to the St. Austells' stoop on the wrong day should warrant me at least one more kiss, shouldn't it?"

Heavens, there was something about him that nearly made her forget her name. The golden hues in his hair, the dark depths of his eyes, perhaps. But it was probably the way he looked at her as though she was the most beautiful girl in the world. "But you said you've forgiven me for that."

"For the wrong date, yes, I suppose I have." He seemed to think for a second. "But I haven't yet forgiven you for upending my phaeton." Then he winked at her. "In fact, I think I may need several dozen kisses to even consider forgiving you for that particular situation."

He would have to mention that! Her cheeks stung a bit. "You are a blackguard, aren't you?"

"Afraid it runs in the family."

∽

There was nothing quite as lovely as Hope Post when she was blushing. If Thad—

"I didn't realize you knew my brother," she said, breaking into his thoughts.

Thad glanced back across the ballroom to find Quentin Post watching them rather closely, and he shrugged. "Actually, I'm well acquainted with both of your brothers."

She blinked up at him, her eyes very close to sparkling, which made Thad's heart twist a bit. What would it take to see the return of that sparkle, full force? He was fairly certain he'd do anything to see it again. She was stunningly beautiful, but when her eyes sparkled...

"Four-in-hand club," he choked out as his voice almost caught in his throat.

"*You* race?" she asked, a smile alighting her face.

Ah, and that smile. Still, she didn't have to sound so

surprised by that fact. He was far from docile himself. "Quentin is easy to defeat. He's often too reckless by half."

She laughed, and the melodic sound reverberated through Thad like nothing ever had. "Met his wife when his horse threw a rock that hit her in the head."

"Why am I not surprised?" Thad laughed right along with her. He could see Quentin Post doing that very thing.

Lady Hope shook her head and her flaxen curls brushed against her shoulders. It was nearly mesmerizing. It would be only too easy to twist one of those curls around his finger, but… He could never do so in Lady St. Austell's ballroom, not with a room full of interested eyes focused on them.

"I would have never taken *you* as a Corinthian, my lord."

"No?" He frowned slightly. "What would you take me as?"

"I thought you were rather frightening when we first met."

"Cruel." He remembered Lady Grace's earlier words at the theatre. "You thought I was cruel."

Lady Hope shrugged. "You *did* bark at Jamie and me, you were quite furious that day."

He had been that. "You could have easily killed my favorite mare. Luckily, Sulis is no worse for the wear."

"And then you told Mr. Lacy I was a menace." Her green eyes focused on him and Thad could happily lose himself in her depths and never want to be found. "I haven't forgiven you for that."

"I did mean to apologize," he began.

Her brow creased in disbelief. "You've had plenty of opportunities, my lord."

He couldn't help but grin as memories of each those opportunities flashed in his mind. "That night at the Wolverlys. I meant to apologize, but you jumped right to the conclusion that I was blackmailing you, and it was so enjoyable, sparring with you, I never did get around to apologizing that night."

"And the next day in the park?"

"You mean after you and your sister tried to pull the wool over my eyes and play me for a fool?" He shook his head just as the first chords of a waltz began. "My dance, I believe."

CHAPTER 10

A fresh wave of tingles raced across Hope as Lord Kilworth drew her into his arms. The heat from his touch nearly singed her, but there was nowhere else she would rather be.

She had the feeling that if they were the only two people in the room, he'd have pulled her closer and kissed her again. How very strange to want him to do so. She'd never thought she'd want anyone to ever kiss her again, not after Henry was gone. But there was something about the earl, something that made her feel…Well, the tiniest bit like her old self.

He led her into a turn, his dark eyes focused so intently on her. "You don't have any sort of inkling who Danby might try to match you with?"

A sennight ago she couldn't have cared less, but that was before she'd careened her way into Lord Kilworth's life. But she couldn't be so forward as to say something like that. "I believe His Grace keeps his own council on all things." How forward could she be, though? "You're not concerned he'll try to foist me upon *you* after seeing us together in the park, are you?"

An enigmatic look flashed in his eyes. Then he leaned in a little closer and said, "Should you decide to foist yourself upon me, I wouldn't complain; but let's do keep Danby out of that, shall we? Not conducive to one's ardor."

Hope couldn't help but laugh. He was so very different than she'd first thought him to be. He did possess the same devilish Baxter nature that Henry once had, though the two of them shared very little else. Learning that he raced was certainly eye-opening. "Are you the sort of fellow who makes wagers, my lord?"

"Wagers?" He quirked one eyebrow as he led her into another turn.

"You know, those foolish things I've heard whispered about. Wagers about which raindrop will reach the bottom of a window pane first. That sort of thing."

"Are you asking if I'm a fool, my lady?"

"Hardly that," she assured him. "I just thought that *we* might have a friendly wager between us, if you'd be willing."

His eyes narrowed slightly as though he was trying to figure her out. "What sort of wager do you have in mind?"

One she had no intention of losing. "Even though they are newly engaged, I wager that Mr. Lacy will not ask my sister to dance even once this evening."

He squinted. "And why would I want to wager about that?"

So she could win, of course. But she shook her head nonchalantly. "Just for amusement, and the opportunity to win a boon from me."

"Mmm." He pulled her a little closer to him. "And *what*, my lady, is it you want from me, should you win?"

Hope grinned up at him. "Well, now that I know how much you love to race, it would be quite delightful to take a team out to the Bath Road, wouldn't it?"

65

"Certainly, you don't think I'd let you drive one of my teams?"

"Well, only if I win the wager."

∼

Her eyes sparkled, just like they had the first time he'd seen her; and Thad stumbled slightly, though he quickly recovered his footing. Heaven help him should she look at him like that on a regular basis. He'd be done for and would never know what hit him. But right in that moment, he was onto her game. "And what if I win?"

The most seductive smile settled on her face and Thad felt it in his groin. "What *would* you want from me, my lord?"

There were many things he wanted, but nothing a gentleman could ask a lady to give him in return for winning a wager. "I suppose I'd like to know where Lacy is this evening." He couldn't help but smile. "It would be very difficult for him to ask Lady Grace to stand up with him if he's not here, wouldn't it?"

Her nose wrinkled up as he'd most definitely caught her, once again, trying to play him. She was utterly charming and matching wits with her was more delightful than he ever would have thought it could be. He splayed his hand across her back and drew her slightly closer once more. She fit so perfectly in arms. Had he made a mistake in telling Danby they wouldn't suit? She might just be the most perfect match he'd ever find, and life with Hope Post would be far from boring.

"You shouldn't hold me so closely," she said softly, though she didn't try to push away from him.

"And you shouldn't attempt to play me for a fool," he teased. "Nor try to get Quentin to remove my head from my shoulders should I take you racing along the Bath Road."

"You're not afraid of *Quent?*" She looked amused at that. "He's much easier to manage than Braden is."

Well, that was probably true. But the man still wouldn't be happy to find out his sister was hell-bent on behaving recklessly. She was docile, his arse. "Be that as it may," he began right as the music came to an end.

The last thing he wanted to do was release her, but there was nothing for it. Thad dropped his hand from her back and released her delicate hand, though he offered her his arm once more.

"We are not racing along the Bath Road," he muttered under his breath.

And she quirked him the most adorable grin. "Afraid you wouldn't be able to keep up?"

Oh, he could keep up with her. He could even show her a few things, and he'd love doing that; but it was hardly appropriate. "My dear—"

A gasp across the room caught his attention as Quentin Post's pretty dark-haired wife collapsed to the floor.

"Oh, good heavens!" Hope released her grasp on Thad's arm. "Lila," she breathed out as she began to push her way through the crowd.

Thad was right behind her.

~

Hope's heart lurched as Quent scooped Lila up in his arms. What in the world had happened? As she reached her family, she felt Lord Kilworth directly behind her. He touched the small of her back and she took a steadying sigh. Who would've thought such a small gesture from him could put her more at ease?

"What happened?" she asked, her gaze darting from Quent to Lila and back.

"Overheated," Quent said, though he didn't sound terribly sure of that. "I do think it's best we leave, love."

"Yes, of course," Hope agreed. Poor Lila. She was such a dear, though Hope suspected her first Season in London must have overtaxed her. Life in Ravenglass was so much more serene than life in Town.

"Thaddeus," Quent said, looking past Hope's shoulder. "Why don't you stop by Post House tomorrow? It's been an age since we've chatted."

Lord Kilworth squeezed Hope's waist with his hand. "Of course," he said evenly. "And, my lady, I do hope you're feeling better soon."

Lila smiled at that, but Quent was glowering. Heavens. Quent rarely glowered. He truly was the more amiable of her brothers. Why in the world did he look so serious and stern?

Hope tipped her head to the side so she could better see the earl. He didn't appear concerned by Quent's glower in the least. In fact, he smiled down at her and offered her his arm. "Happy to escort you to your coach."

CHAPTER 11

Thad waited until the Post carriage departed before turning back into the St. Austells' foyer, wondering what in the world had gotten into him. When he'd first come to Town this Season, he'd been singularly focused on getting a new church building bill passed in parliament, but after meeting Lady Hope…Well, he'd quickly become quite focused on her instead.

Thoughts about a broken phaeton, one Earth-shattering kiss, and an amazing waltz were all and overshadowed by the threat of Danby and his special licenses, and *now* Quentin Post seemed quite ready to stick his head on a pike.

He started back towards the ballroom, even though there was no reason for him to remain at the St. Austells' now that Hope had left. Just as he was about to pass an open parlor—

"Oh, Truscott, you did miss it!" laughed one gentleman from inside the room. "You should have seen Kilworth just now."

Thad's eyes widened. He never really listened at doors. But he *had* heard his name, so he stopped right outside the parlor.

"Picking right up where his cousin left off," another fellow said with merriment lacing his voice.

"Lady Hope?" Charles Truscott sounded amused.

"One wonders," the first gentleman continued, "do you think she only lifts her skirts for Baxter men, or might she lift them for me too?"

A muscle twitched in Thad's jaw.

"Oh, I shouldn't think it would take too much effort," the second fellow replied. "Probably a natural reflex at this point."

While the three men laughed at Hope's expense, Thad's blood began to pound in his veins. The veritable jackasses. Hope might be somewhat reckless, which if he was honest was one of the things he loved about her, but…Dear God, did he actually love her? Had he truly fallen completely in love with Hope Post?

"Not like the other one," the first gentleman said. Who was that? Hessenford? Sounded like his voice. The degenerate. "Odds are Lacy's cock will freeze off on his wedding night."

"If he makes it that far," Truscott said. "I'd lay even odds Prestwood kills the man before he ever says 'I do'. In fact, he should probably make sure his will is in order, just to be on the safe side."

"It won't even take any time at all," the second fellow added. "He'll leave everything to his bastard sister anyway, even *your* brother could draw it up for him with very little effort."

The obnoxious trio laughed again. Weren't they the three most charming arses in all of Britain? Was there anyone they didn't disparage?

"Wonder if I shouldn't try to steal the Post chit away from Kilworth," Hessenford said. "Wouldn't mind having her legs wrapped around me even if Henry Baxter did get there first."

"Well," Truscott began, but Thad wasn't about to let any of them say another word.

He strode right into the parlor and surveyed the trio – Charles Truscott, the ne'er-do-well youngest son of Lord Holsworthy; Viscount Hessenford, a debauched rake along the same lines as Henry had been; and John Pearce, the nephew and heir presumptive of the Marquess of Calverleigh – each of them lounged in chairs, drinking some of St. Austell's brandy, by the looks of their glasses.

"Evening," Thad said, sounding much more amiable than he felt at the moment.

Only Pearce had the decency to look slightly uncomfortable by Thad's sudden appearance. "Kilworth," he muttered in greeting.

"I couldn't quite help but overhear you mentioning Lady Hope just now."

Hessenford smirked. "Listening at doorways these days? I wouldn't have thought you were the sort."

"Happenstance, I assure you." Thad clasped his hands behind his back, which kept him from balling his hand into a fist. Pummeling the man in Lady St. Austell's parlor would not bode well for anyone, most especially Hope.

"If you say so." The viscount picked at an invisible piece of lint on his jacket, unaware or unconcerned about the fury coursing through Thad. Condescending jackass.

"Tell me, do I strike you as the sort who would defend a lady on a field of honor, Hessenford? Because that is where we're headed."

That got the viscount's attention and he glanced back up at Thad. "I hardly think a dawn appointment over a bit o' muslin is necessary, old man."

A bit o' muslin? Thad would only be too glad to put a ball in Hessenford's black heart. "Afraid I must disagree with you," he said evenly. "Lady Hope's honor has been besmirched and I cannot let that stand." He glanced from Truscott to Pearce. "I assume one of you will serve as his second."

Pearce looked as though he might be ill.

"If you insist on this," Truscott grumbled, "I suppose it would be me."

"Perfect." Thad nodded in the man's direction. "I'm naming Robert Cole as mine. I'm certain you can find him at Whites this evening to work out the details. See you in the morning."

CHAPTER 12

*H*eavens! What was that?

Something awful must be going on below. Quent had let out a bark of anger, the likes of which Hope had never heard before. At least, she assumed it was Quent. Her brother was very rarely angry about anything, but it *did* sound like him.

Hope scrambled from her bed and opened her door. She found Grace in the corridor too as though her slumber had also been broken by the sound below. "What was that?" her sister whispered.

Hope shrugged as she tightened her wrap about her waist, then she and her sister padded down the steps and started towards the white parlor.

"I knew it. I knew it when I saw him tonight this wouldn't end well. I just don't understand what she could possibly have done in so short a time that would result in *this*!" Quent's furious voice echoed down the hall.

Hope and Grace stopped where they stood and exchanged a glance with each other. What in the world had happened?

73

"Alcott didn't say," came Lord Wolverly's voice. "Honestly, he probably doesn't know. It's not as though fellows spill their souls to him about these sorts of things. They just need his services."

Doctor Alcott? Lord Wolverly's brother-in-law?

"Well what *does* he know?" Quent boomed.

"Just what I've told you. Lord Robert sought him out and asked him to be present in the morning should either Kilworth or Hessenford be injured…"

Should *Kilworth* be injured? Hope gasped as her hand fluttered to her chest. Why in the world would Lord Kilworth be injured? Grace frowned at her, but Hope didn't know anything more than her sister did.

"But it sounds like the whole thing has something to do with Hope's honor. I just thought you should be aware."

It had to do with *her* honor? Hope's knees nearly buckled beneath her. What in the world had happened?

And then her brother stood in the doorway of the parlor, his face red and his hazel eyes flashing with anger. "Eavesdropping now, are you?"

Hope shook her head.

"Hardly," Grace said waspishly. "Who would need to? You could wake the dead with your bellowing."

Quent sucked in a breath and was about to lose his temper which wouldn't help anything. "Why might Lord Kilworth be injured?" Hope asked quickly.

Her brother focused his attention on her. "I'd like to ask you the same thing. What did you do that would inspire the man to challenge Hessenford in order to defend you?"

A duel? Of all the stupid, ridiculous, foolish, dangerous… Hope thought she might be ill, but she managed to shake her head. "On my word, I've done nothing, Quent." She barely even knew Lord Hessenford. In fact, she wasn't certain if she'd even spoken with the viscount all Season. Oh, dear heavens, what if something happened to Lord Kilworth? What if he was injured? What if…What if he was killed? A chill washed over her. After Henry, she couldn't…

"Kilworth challenged Hessenford?" Grace asked. "I don't see how that could have anything to do with Hope."

Quent glared at their sister. "I didn't ask you."

But Grace shook her head most stubbornly. "She was in the ballroom all evening at the St. Austells', as were we all. There's nothing she could have done, Quentin."

"Yes, well, none of it is any of *your* concern," Quent clipped out, then gestured to their general state. "You're hardly dressed to entertain guests. Go back to bed, both of you."

He couldn't honestly think she could just go back to bed! What if something happened to Lord Kilworth? What if when she awoke he'd been killed? She'd already lost one man she loved and…She couldn't *love* Lord Kilworth, could she? She liked him was all. She hadn't at first, but she did now. She liked his kisses, she liked how she felt in his arms, she even liked bantering with him, not that she'd ever tell him that. But she liked him a great deal, and if he somehow died trying to defend her honor… "Quent, you can't let him do this," she whispered. "Can't you stop it? Can't you do something?"

Her brother heaved a sigh and shook his head. "There's not a thing I can do about it, love. He could come to his senses by morning and call the whole thing off, I suppose. But if either of those men are injured or killed and it has something to do with you, I don't know how you'll ever survive it. After last year…"

"Can't you talk to him?" She didn't care one whit about whether or not she survived the scandal of it. Her future wasn't one she could control anyway, but if something should happen to Lord Kilworth, she didn't think she could survive *that*. "Make him see reason? Quent, can't—"

"Do you *care* about the man?" Quent asked, his eyes softening just a bit.

"He's quite wonderful," she admitted. Oh, heavens, panic seized her heart again! What if something happened to him? "Please, can't you talk to him?"

Her brother heaved a sigh. "I'll head to Green Park beforehand and see if I can get him to change his mind, but there're no guarantees, love."

Hope sagged slightly from relief. "Thank you for trying."

Then she turned slowly and started back for the stairs with her sister beside her. Together they climbed the steps and once they'd reached the top, Grace whispered, "You really didn't do anything, did you?"

Hope shook her head. "You're the one who said I was docile this Season." But perhaps it was time to stop being docile. What if Quent wasn't able to get Lord Kilworth to see reason? What if he stubbornly dueled Lord Hessenford and ended up getting himself killed? She couldn't let that happen. Being docile was for the birds. "But now you have to help me sneak out."

Grace looked at her as though she'd lost her mind, and perhaps she had. "I beg your pardon?"

"He might not listen to Quent," she stressed, "but he'll listen to me. If I can just see him…"

"You're bound for Bedlam, do you know that?"

"Wouldn't you risk everything to save Mr. Lacy?"

Grace frowned slightly at that and shrugged. "Mama will have both of our heads if she finds out. You'll be ruined."

But with Grace helping her, no one would ever find out. There was no one she trusted as well as she did Grace, her most clever sister and the most ardent secret keeper in the family. "We'll just have to make sure that doesn't happen then."

Hope needed to change clothes, sneak down the back steps to the kitchen and escape into the mews. The most dangerous part would be making her way from South Audley Street to Upper Brook Street this time of night by herself, but as long as she was careful, she could manage to go unseen. And once at Baxter House, she'd have to talk some sense into Lord Kilworth. She prayed he'd listen.

∼

"You're a damned fool," Robert said, dropping onto the settee across from Thad's chair.

"Yes, you've said that at least a dozen times this evening." Even so, his friend had done his duty in establishing a set of rules of conduct for his dawn appointment with Hessenford.

"Well, it's a new day, so my tally can start over." Robert scrubbed a hand down his face.

It was *technically* a new day, but Thad wouldn't get any sleep until after he'd met the degenerate viscount at Green Park. Much better just to stay up than risk being groggy from disturbed sleep. "He's a rotten shot, isn't he?"

He thought, after all, he'd remembered hearing that some time ago. Something about missing his target during an entire hunting party, something like that.

"Ahem!" His butler Morris cleared his throat. "There is a, um, young lady, my lord. I—" he stammered, looking more than uncomfortable. "Well, she's asking for you."

"You can't be serious," Robert grumbled.

Thad pushed out of his seat and frowned at his friend. A *young lady*? What in the world? He brushed past his butler into the corridor and there in the foyer, all dressed in black, was Lady Hope. She looked like she was in mourning.

"What in God's name?" he asked. Honestly, had she lost her mind? The last place in the world she should be at this hour was at his home. Didn't she have any sort of care for her reputation?

"Please don't do this, my lord," she said, her voice catching slightly in her throat.

Thad closed the distance between them, and against his better judgment, he pulled her into his arms. "Hope," he breathed out. "What *are* you doing here?" He was, after all, trying to protect her good name and she was tossing it aside just as quickly with both hands.

She tilted her head back to better see him. "Tell me you won't do this, please tell me you won't."

He released a breath. She knew. Somehow she'd found out about the duel, that much was obvious. He had no idea how she could have found out, but the how didn't matter at the moment. "If you're worried for my safety, there's no reason," he tried to assure her. And there wasn't any reason. He was a decent shot. He always had been. Much better than Hessenford, in any event.

Tears pooled in her eyes, and the sight tugged at his heart. "I couldn't bear it if something happened to you," she whispered. "I can't lose you too. Please, my lord."

And the urge to console her and soothe her washed over him, and before he knew it, he'd cupped her face and kissed her. She pressed up on her toes as though to get closer to him which drove him half-mad with want. Thad pulled her closer to him and deepened their kiss. She tasted of sweetness and innocence and everything Thad ever wanted in life.

She clung to his jacket, pulling him closer, and sighed against his lips. He delved inside the haven of her mouth and tangled his tongue with hers. Dear God, she'd be the death of him. Holding her, kissing her, feeling her curves pressed against him…The last thing Thad wanted was to ever lose her.

He wanted to feel her skin against his, he wanted to kiss and taste every inch of her, and he wanted her in his bed now and for always. He pressed her against the door and his hands dropped to her waist. She kissed him back with fervor, and a groan escaped him. If he could just get—

"We, uh, should probably be getting to the field," Robert said from somewhere behind them.

And Thad winced as he lifted his head. Damn it all! Why did Robert have to come upon them *now*? Hope blinked up at him in surprise.

"Give me a moment, Rob." He blew out a breath.

Then he waited until he heard his friend's footsteps retreat before he took Hope's hand and tugged her down the corridor to his study. He'd been a damned fool to keep her in the foyer where anyone could stumble upon them.

Once they crossed the threshold, he pressed his lips to her forehead. "Stay here, I'll be right back."

Then he made his way to his parlor to find his friend frowning at him as though he was the worst sort of villain. "Have you lost your mind? Has *she*?"

It was quite possible they both had lost their minds, not that Thad was about to admit as much to Robert Cole. "Pretend you never saw her here, all right?"

Robert snorted. "I'm not your problem, Thad. What are the odds no one else saw her?"

It *was* nearly dawn. Someone could have seen her as they'd come home from whatever event they'd attended that night. Robert was right. That was a problem. "She came to talk me out of the duel."

"Well, in that case, I'm sure no one will care then about the propriety of her showing up on your doorstep in the middle of the night." His friend shook his head. "You'd best not put a ball in Hessenford's heart and exile yourself. She'll be well and thoroughly ruined then."

She was well and thoroughly ruined now, but…Well, she wouldn't be for long. "I'll meet you at Green Park in less than an hour."

"Does she even have an honor to defend?" Robert asked as he started for the threshold.

"Ask that again and you'll find yourself on the other end of my pistol next."

His friend sighed. "Just think about what you're doing, Thad. At one time you were the smartest friend I had."

He was still smart, he'd just lost his heart to a less-than docile girl and she brought out a recklessness in him. Someday Robert would understand. Perhaps. There wasn't, after all, another girl in the whole world like Hope Post, even if there were two girls who looked just like her. "I'll see you in less than an hour," he said again. Then Thad left the parlor and started for his study once more.

There was really only one thing he could do, and while he'd initially rejected the idea, he didn't have a choice any longer. Not only was it the best course of action to take, the whole thing didn't frighten him as much as he would have thought. In fact, he rather thought he'd enjoy it.

∾

Hope was trembling as she paced the earl's study, stopping at his mahogany desk as the last few minutes washed over her. Heavens! She hadn't even considered that Lord Kilworth might have a visitor at this hour. Now that she thought about it, the earl could have already been in bed when she'd arrived on his doorstep. But he hadn't been in bed. He'd been wide awake and the way he'd kissed her…Well, she was likely to faint just thinking about it.

"Hope," Lord Kilworth said from the threshold, and she spun around to face him.

His dark eyes were focused on her and her breath caught in her throat. No man had ever looked at her that way, not even Henry.

"You *do* realize it was reckless to come here?" he asked, clasping his hands behind his back.

"I *had* to see you." She grasped onto the back of his desk to keep herself upright. "I had to talk to you. You can't do this, my lord. Please tell me you'll cancel this nonsense."

A muscle twitched in his jaw. "It's not nonsense, Hope, and you shouldn't even know anything about it."

But she did know about it. And he had to see reason. "My lord—"

"Thaddeus," he corrected. "From now on, anyway."

"Thaddeus?" She tested his name on her tongue and a thrill raced through her.

"Or Thad," he said, and closed the distance between them. He took her waist in both of his hands and pulled her against him.

Heavens, he was strong. His chest was hard as a marble against her breasts. Hope swallowed nervously "Thad," she whispered, staring up into his eyes.

He smiled. "It's too dangerous for anyone to see you leave here, Hope. So wait for me here until I'm finished with Hessenford and I'll be back as soon as I can."

He was mad. She couldn't stay *here*. For one thing, Grace would be beside herself with worry, waiting for Hope to come home. And for another, she hadn't come here to *wait* for him. She'd come to talk sense into him. "Thad, you can't meet Hessenford. You can't. If something happened to you—"

"And *when* I come back," he continued as though she hadn't spoken at all, "we'll send for your family and a vicar or rector, whoever's available and be married in my front parlor."

She could not have heard him correctly. Hope blinked up at him. "Be *married*?"

He nodded once and a bit of his golden hair fell across his brow. "We might as well put one of Danby's special licenses to use." He winked at her. "I won't have anyone speak ill of you, Hope. Not Hessenford, not anyone who might have spotted you tonight, and—"

"No one saw me," she protested. "I was very careful and I wore the darkest dress I have."

"Robert Cole saw you," he said matter-of-factly. There was the strangest twinkle in his eyes. "Tell me again why you came here tonight."

"To see you, to talk to you, to make certain—"

"You said you couldn't *lose* me." His voice rumbled over her.

A shiver raced through Hope, and she dropped her gaze to his cravat, embarrassed that she'd admitted as much to him, even if it was true.

"I told you I saw Danby about his special licenses."

He had said that at the St. Austells'. Hope nodded.

"I have no idea who he plans to match you with, Hope. But I can't lose you either." His hands squeezed possessively at her waist. "I'm not certain how or when it happened, but I am quite in love with you."

Hope's heart lifted, and she tilted her head back to meet his eyes. Oh, good heavens! She wasn't sure how it had happened either. But it had. Somehow. "I love you too," she whispered with a shake of her head, almost surprised to hear those words come out of her mouth.

"Then it's settled," he said and then dipped his head down to kiss her once more.

But it wasn't settled, and Hope pushed at his chest, which

seemed to ripple beneath her fingertips. "I won't marry you, not if you meet Hessenford."

His mouth dropped open like he couldn't imagine that she would ever say such a thing. "Are we negotiating again?"

She'd do anything she had to in order to keep him alive.

"I will not negotiate your future, Hope. I will not negotiate your reputation. As your husband, you'll always know that I'll protect you, that you'll be safe. That's *why* I have to meet Hessenford."

"And what about you?" she choked out. "Who will keep *you* safe?"

His brow lifted as though she'd offended him. "So little faith in my abilities?"

That wasn't what she meant at all, but the fact of the matter was Hessenford *would* have a pistol pointed at Thad. It wasn't a terribly safe place to put oneself. He had to see that. "I just don't want to put your life at risk, not for me."

And then he smiled once more and brushed his fingers against her cheeks. "There's no one else I would risk everything for, Hope. But you need to trust me. I do know what I'm doing."

Did he? Did he know more than she did about this sort of thing? Well, probably. Ladies didn't go around dueling with each other when they were offended. They gave each other the cut direct or gossiped behind each other's backs, which wasn't terribly nice; but it wasn't lethal.

"You could call the whole thing off. *You* challenged him."

He blew out a breath. "You do realize this is precisely why ladies should be kept in the dark as far as duels and matters of honor go, do you not?"

Did that mean he was weakening? Hope batted her lashes at him, the same way she'd seen Lila do with Quent. It usually worked for her sister-in-law. "I shall never involve myself again…assuming my husband isn't involved himself, of course."

He laughed as he shook his head. "I will give Hessenford the opportunity to apologize, Hope. If he does so, I'll withdraw my challenge. Wedding gift to my bride."

She threw her arms around his neck and held him tight. Heavens! Who would have ever thought a crash of phaetons in Hyde Park would lead to…this, to her finding that part of her she thought had died, to finding a gentleman who was so perfect for her in every way, to a future she never could have hoped for.

CHAPTER 13

*G*reen Park was blanketed in fog as Thad entered the gates on Sulis' back. He smoothed a hand across his mare's neck, urging her towards the silhouette of a carriage in the distance. That had to be Doctor Alcott's coach. Everyone else would arrive on horseback just like he was.

The closer they got to the carriage, Thad started to make out figures, four of them. He must be the last to arrive. But he wouldn't have changed the last few minutes at Baxter House for anything in the world, not with Hope in his arms and kissing him with every bit of passion she possessed. And when he got home, and after some vicar named them husband and wife, he was going to do a lot more than just kiss his new countess. In fact, they may not be seen for days. Or perhaps not for the rest of the Season. They could head right to Chivelesword Abbey. Of course, his mother would want to meet Hope; but he'd rather not detour through Yorkshire if he didn't have to. Mother could probably be convinced to visit Leicestershire in a few months or so. By then, Hope would have the run of the place.

Robert waved his arm in the air to catch Thad's notice, and…What the devil? Was that *Quentin Post* standing right beside his friend? Damn it all, he hadn't planned on seeing Hope's brother at this engagement. Was the man likely to call Thad out right after he dispensed with Hessenford? His stomach knotted. Was Post looking for Hope? Had he realized she'd gone missing in the dead of night?

Thad pulled back on Sulis' reins, and his mare came to stop before the four men. Robert Cole, Quentin Post, Doctor Alcott, and Charles Truscott. So, then, where the devil was Hessenford?

Thad surveyed the foursome and then dismounted. "Where's Hessenford? Hiding somewhere?" That seemed like the coward. He'd make the worst sort of remarks about Hope and then fail to show.

"Um, well," Robert stammered, looking rather uncomfortable.

"Since my services are *not* needed," Doctor Alcott began, "I'll be returning home."

Since his services weren't needed? What in the world? "Where *is* Hessenford?" Thad asked again.

"Dead," Truscott said, sounding quite dismayed and more than a little stunned.

"Dead?" Thad echoed, louder than was necessary. How was that even possible?

Alcott was either uninterested in the story or had already heard it. The doctor turned his back on the group and started for his coach.

"He apparently visited Madam Dubois' tonight," Robert said, glancing towards Truscott as though making certain he had the story right.

"He was foxed," the viscount's second added, shaking his head.

The man *had* been properly soused when Thad saw him at St. Austells'.

"Didn't take his trousers completely off," Robert continued. "Tripped over his own feet and…"

"Crashed his head against the bedpost," Truscott continued.

"And died?" Thad asked, not quite believing such a thing. The man, foxed as he was at the St, Austells', had seemed in perfect health. He'd cracked his head on a bedpost at a bawdy house? Fitting as that was…

"Well, at first the whore…er…*girl,*" Truscott amended quickly, "At first she thought he'd just been knocked unconscious and was sleeping off the blue ruin he'd downed, but…" He shrugged. "I don't know how long he was really dead. I'm assuming you don't want me to stand in for him. I'm happy to apologize for the uncomplimentary things that were said about Lady Hope tonight if—"

"What exactly *were* those things?" Quentin Post snapped. "You might be off the hook with Kilworth, but as the lady is my sister."

But the lady was about to be Thad's wife. How was Quentin Post going to take that news? Would he call Thad out himself over the matter? Perhaps Alcott shouldn't hurry away, after all.

"I'm certain Mr. Truscott and Mr. Pearce imbibed so much this evening they won't be able to recall the conversation," Thad said, wanting to be done with Truscott altogether. "And they'll never mention it in the future."

Truscott nodded quickly. "Absolutely, Kilworth. We have only the upmost respect for Lady Hope."

"I am glad to hear that," Quentin growled, sounding fiercer than Thad had ever heard him.

Damn it all, he was going to have to tell the man that Hope was currently at Baxter House. It would have been so much easier to do so in a note, summoning all of the Post family together for an impromptu wedding. Quentin's wife did, after all, seem to have a calming effect on the man. But there was nothing for it. Post was here and his wife was not.

Thad gestured towards a nearby copse with a tip of his head. "Mind if I have a word with you?"

Quentin's hazel gaze narrowed on Thad. "I believe we are overdue for that."

Thad took a steadying breath and lifted Sulis' reins towards Robert. "Do you mind?"

His friend took the reins and cast him an expression that seemed to wish him luck. And he could use every bit of luck available to him. Quentin Post was amiable most of the time, but…Well, this was hardly a usual situation.

"Hear me out before you try to kill me," Thad said once they'd reached the copse of trees.

Quentin frowned, looking Thad up and down. "You think that's the best way to start this conversation?"

Well, it would be nice to acquire that promise before Thad went any further. "Hope is at Baxter House right now."

"I beg your pardon?" Who knew Quentin's frown could darken?

Thad heaved a sigh. "She wanted to talk me out of the whole Hessenford duel."

"The little idiot." Her brother looked pained as he closed his eyes and scrubbed a hand down his face. "It's as though she's hell-bent on ruining herself."

"It's very possible someone spotted her," Thad agreed. "So I told her to stay there until I finished here to keep anyone else from seeing her, but—"

Quentin's eyes opened again. "But…?" he prodded.

Best just to say it. After all, it would soften the blow, right? "I love her, Quentin. This isn't the way I would have gone about all of this if I'd had the choice, but things being what they are, that decision has been taken out of my hands."

Post's eyes focused even more intently on Thad, silently studying him. At least he wasn't calling him out. That could only be a good sign.

"I've asked her to marry me. I think we should do so this morning at Baxter House. We'd like your family present, of course. But the sooner we're wed, the better for her."

"You love her?" he asked. "You're certain?"

Thad was quite that, and he nodded in response. "Very."

"And you won't let her run wild anymore?"

"She won't be walking the streets of Mayfair in the dead of night to visit gentleman's homes," Thad replied, though he didn't want to tame Hope. He loved the energy she possessed, her spirit, even her recklessness, as long as it was directed properly. Heaven forbid she become more docile.

"In that case—" Quentin reached inside his greatcoat and pulled out a piece of paper "—this is for you."

Thad took the paper from the fellow and glanced down at it. A special license, with his name and Hope's written in a very familiar hand. A chill raced through him. "Danby?" he asked in awe.

For the first time that night, Quentin smiled. "One of his men delivered that after we'd returned from St. Austell's a few hours ago."

But that didn't even seem possible. Thad returned his attention to the license in his hand. "How in the world could he have known—"

A snort escaped Quentin. "Over the last year, I have come to believe His Grace knows all things. Only a fool would get on the wrong side of him."

That was a very good point. Thad pocketed the license and shook his head. "So perhaps we should get married in the afternoon instead. Give His Grace time to attend the ceremony." One that the duke had inexplicably known would take place.

"That does seem a good plan," Quentin agreed. "I'll bring Vicar Wright, shall I?"

Thad nodded. "That would be most appreciated."

CHAPTER 14

*H*ope couldn't sit still. Anxiety coursed through her veins and she alternated from sitting on Thad's settee to crossing the room and back more times than she could count. Shouldn't he be back by now? If he'd called off the duel, shouldn't he be back? Waiting for his return felt like an eternity.

What if Hessenford hadn't apologized? What if the duel proceeded and Thad was bleeding in the middle of Green Park? Or worse? If only there was a way to know for sure. She could ask the butler – Morris, wasn't it? - to have Thad's carriage brought around and go to the park herself. What if he couldn't move and was bleeding, lifeless on the ground?

She couldn't let him suffer like that!

Hope started for the corridor to summon the butler and—

The air whooshed out of her as she bumped right into Thaddeus Baxter!

Oh! She'd never been more relieved about anything in her life. "Thank heavens!" She threw her arms around his neck and breathed in the scent of him – morning dew, horses and his citric shaving lotion. Nothing had ever smelled so wonderful. "I was so worried."

Thad tipped her chin up and looked down at her, an enigmatic look in his dark eyes. "With good reason. Your brother was there. I thought it quite likely he'd try to remove my head."

Drat! She'd forgotten all about Quent! "Oh, Thad! I'm so sorry. Was he awful? What did he say? What happened with Hessenford? You're not hurt, are you? Did he apologize? What—"

"Take a breath." He chuckled. Then he led her back to the settee where she'd waited a lifetime for him to return. He'd vowed he was uninjured and explained about Hessenford's sudden death. He told her about Danby's special license, and Quent promising to bring her mother and sister to Baxter House that afternoon to see them wed, and that he'd bring Vicar Wright along with him.

"Lord Prestwood's cousin?" she asked in surprise. "I hadn't realized he was in London."

Thad yawned. "I've never met the man, but as long as he can perform the ceremony, I don't really care."

Hope squeezed his hand. "You're exhausted."

"It has been some time since I slept."

The same was true for her too. She smiled at the handsome earl. "Go get some sleep. I promise not to get into any trouble in your absence."

But he shook his head. "Oh, I don't think I'll dare let you out of my sight, my love." Then he slid an arm beneath her knees and scooped her up in his arms.

Heavens! Hope squealed in surprise. "What are you doing?" she asked as she wrapped her arms around his neck to keep from sliding off his lap.

"I'm about to make love to you," he replied, pushing off

the settee and starting for the threshold. "You'll be my wife in a few hours anyway."

Was he serious? Right now in the middle of the day? Didn't people do that sort of thing in the dark? And after they were married? He was as reckless as she was, wasn't he? Hope's heart thudded against her chest. What if someone found out? But they *would* be man and wife in just a few hours. "I thought you needed to rest."

"I need you more," he said low, making a thrill race through her.

Hope stared up into Thad's eyes and a sigh escaped her. This man, this handsome earl she'd hated on sight, was her perfect match. How in the world had that happened?

∽

Her light wisteria scent swirled around Thad as he climbed the stairs with his bride-to-be in his arms; and he couldn't wait to bury his head against her skin and breathe her in.

She giggled. "Don't you dare drop me, Thaddeus."

"Never," he vowed. "Not in a million years." Dropping her would put a rather quick end to how he wanted to spend the rest of his morning. And ever since he'd walked back into Baxter House, he had very specific plans for how he wanted the rest of his day to go. He wasn't about to take any chances that Quentin Post or the dowager Marchioness of Bradenham, really, would find some other way around this situation. And he didn't want to lose Hope, he couldn't lose her.

He stalked down the corridor towards his chambers and nudged the door wider with his boot. Luckily there was no one about and he closed the door firmly behind them. He placed her gently beside his bed and shrugged out of his jacket.

"Need help with your buttons?"

Hope turned her back to him and tossed her blonde locks over one shoulder as Thad slid the row of pearl buttons through their holes. He tugged the dark velvet from her skin and placed his lips on the back of her neck. He couldn't help but sigh. Her light scent teased him, the softness of her skin entranced him and her gentle intake of breath drew him closer.

He pulled her against his chest and his stiff cock pressed against her rounded bottom. Damn it all, he'd be lucky if he could get his trousers off with out spilling himself inside them.

"No regrets in becoming the Countess of Kilworth," he rasped near her ear. Goosebumps spread across her skin and Thad dipped his head to kiss them away.

Hope shook her head. "No regrets."

"None in becoming *my* countess?" She had, after all, once wanted that title when his cousin had been the earl.

She spun in his arms and her green eyes sparkled just as they had last night during their waltz. That enchanting sparkle he hadn't known she still possessed until last night. But there it was, sparkling at him. His heart thudded, waiting for her answer. "I meant what I said this morning, Thad. I *do* love you. And I can't wait to be your countess in name and reality."

And that was all he needed to hear.

Thad tugged at his cravat and his waistcoat followed it onto the floor in a heap. He leaned forward and captured her lips with his. He let his fingers trail up her middle and stop at her breasts that he'd wanted to touch since that very first day he'd seen her dripping wet beside the Serpentine.

He squeezed her with both hands and smiled when she sighed against his lips. "Ah, my little vixen, you're all mine now."

She pulled back slightly. "Not quite yet, my lord."

She was my lording him? Now? Right next to his bed? Thad's eyes widened.

"How would you feel about a little wager?"

Oh dear God, she was going to be the death of him. "You want to go riding along the Bath Road?" he guessed aloud. He'd take her anywhere she wanted just as long as she removed her dress.

She grinned so seductively, Thad's cock twitched in response. "Well, only if I win."

Oh, he was going to enjoy spending his life with her. "And what is the wager, my dear Hope?"

"I'd wager that being your wife will make me the happiest girl in all the world."

Well, he didn't want to take the opposite side in *that* wager. "And you think I'd bet against that?"

Her eyes sparkled once more and she shook her head. "Best if you just concede to me that you'll take me racing along the Bath Road."

And anything else in the world she ever wanted. Thad nodded once in agreement. "Now, darling, do take off that dress and make *me* the happiest man in all the world, will you?"

Hope tugged one sleeve of her dress, making her bodice gape and Thad couldn't pull his eyes from her. Then she slid her other arm through and her dark gown dropped to her waist. He could make out her dusky nipples peaking beneath her chemise. Dear God...

Thad untied the ribbons of her chemise and somehow managed not to groan as her clothing slid down her waist, pooling at their feet. She was more beautiful than he'd imagined and he'd imagined her many times since he'd first spotted her in the Serpentine that day.

He reached one hand out and brushed the pad of this

thumb against one of her nipples. When she sucked in a quick breath, he couldn't take anymore. Thad groaned and then pulled his shirt over his head.

∽

Hope's eyes widened at seeing the muscles she'd only felt beneath his superfine. Heavens, he was magnificent. She tentatively reached out to touch the dusting of golden hair on his chest. Thad sucked in a breath as her fingertips grazed his flattened nipples. She swallowed nervously. She'd never seen a man's bare chest before, and…Well, he *was* a masterpiece that could have been carved out of marble.

Thad leaned forward and kissed her again. Anticipation skittered down her spine when he untied the ribbon of her drawers. He kissed her deeper, plundering her mouth. Hope wrapped her arms around his neck to keep her legs from buckling beneath her.

And then he once again scooped her up in his arms and placed her gently in the middle of his bed. Quickly, he tossed one, then two boots across the room and then started on the buttons of his trousers.

Hope pressed up on her elbows, watching him with great fascination as he slid his trousers over his hips and…Well, she'd never seen anything like *that* and her mouth went a little dry. Heavens, she had no idea what she was supposed to do.

Luckily, he did seem to know. After tossing his trousers aside, Thad gently opened her legs and kissed his way from one knee to the apex of her thighs…and then he kissed her there too.

Hope sucked in a breath as his tongue pressed against her and then pushed inside her. Never in her life had she ever felt anything like that. "Thad!"

He chuckled against her flesh, but continued to kiss and lick her until she was grasping the bedclothes with both hands and writhing beneath him. Then he pushed up to his knees and settled himself between hers. His dark gaze nearly scorched her. "My stunning countess."

Her cheeks warmed, which was silly. She was lying there, after all, completely bare for his gaze, but his words made her blush?

Thad took his manhood in his hand and pressed the tip of him against her wetness. How foreign that felt but amazingly wonderful at the same time, and all she wanted was for him to be closer to touch that place deep inside her that throbbed.

"Put your legs around me, Hope," he whispered.

When she did, he pushed further into her and then with a quick thrust of his hips, he was completely inside her. Hope gasped at the slight pain that wrought within her.

"Sorry, darling." He kissed her neck. "It won't be like that again."

She smacked his back. "You knew that would hurt?"

Thad pushed up to look at her. "That's my understanding with virgins, but it won't hurt again."

Hope narrowed her eyes on him. "Anything else you're neglecting to tell me, Thaddeus?"

He shook his head and his golden hair fell across his brow. "Come now, you're the girl who swims in the Serpentine and topples over phaetons, certainly you can handle a twinge of pain."

"Says the man who didn't feel any pain, at all," she complained.

A broad smile spread across his face. "My love, I have been in pain every night since I met you."

That was hardly complimentary. "What is that supposed to mean?"

He dipped his head down and pressed his lips to hers

once more. "It means," he began softly, "that the need to have you in my bed was so intense it was painful to walk sometimes."

Well, she supposed that was a *little* complimentary, then. Thad pulled slightly from her and then thrust inside her again, but slower this time and filling her so completely that heat coursed through her. His hand settled on her breast and he kneaded her as he kissed her even deeper.

A moan escaped Hope and her eyes fluttered closed. Thad retreated and then pressed further inside her, over and over, finding a rhythm that might drive her mad. A pressure began to build inside her, and his pace increased.

Heavens!

Hope settled her hands on his back and loved the feel of his muscles beneath her fingertips. He kissed her harder and that pressure in her core increased and then…

And then…

Hope cried out as she fell over an edge she hadn't known was there. A half second later, Thad grasped her waist in his hands and let out a cry of his own. Then he collapsed on top of her and buried his face in her hair.

"I love how you smell," he whispered.

Hope thumped him on the back. "I thought you were going to say you loved *me*."

Thad pushed back up on his arms, the dark blue in his depths twinkling devilishly. "Give me a moment to recover and I'll show you how much I love you all over again."

CHAPTER 15

*T*had thought he heard a scratch at the door, but he was too tired to know for certain. Hope murmured something in her sleep against his chest, and he tightened his hold on her. The softness of her skin against his fingers lulled him back to sleep until...

That was *definitely* a scratch.

Damn it all. "Yes?" he managed to croak out. If he could just sleep for a couple days...

"Lord Kilworth," Morris called through the door. "You have visitors."

Visitors? Thad's eyes flew open. What the devil? What time was it?

"Just a moment, Morris." Thad slid from beneath Hope and tossed his discarded shirt back on, which thankfully covered his nether regions. Then he padded across the floor and opened his door just a crack. "Who's here?" he whispered.

His poor butler looked more than uncomfortable. "Everyone, sir."

"You're going to have to be more specific than that, Morris."

His servant released a sigh. "The Duke of Danby, Mr. and Mrs. Buswell—"

Sarah and Lawrence were there?

"—Lady Bradenham, Lord Quentin, Lady Quentin, Lady Grace, Lord Robert—"

Morris was right. Everyone was there.

"—and a Mr. Wright."

The vicar. Damn it! He and Hope must've slept the morning away. "Tell them we'll be right down—"No that would never do, not with his sister present. She'd think Hope awful the rest of her days. "I mean, tell them I'm finishing up something in my study and you'll have someone wake Lady Hope from her nap."

"Very good, my lord."

Thad shut the door and then turned back to the bed where Hope was still sleeping, her flaxen curls spread out across his bed. He could stare at her like that for a lifetime and never tire of the sight. But not now, not while... Did Morris say *Danby* was there too?

"Hope love," he said crossing the floor and dropping onto the edge of his four-poster. "Sweetheart." He brushed a hand across her cheek. "Your family's here."

Her eyes popped open. "My family?"

"Mmm. Let's get you dressed, shall we?"

∽

Hope's hands were shaking, her stomach was plummeting and her heart was beating a mile a minute. Not a peep came from within the parlor. That couldn't be good, could it? Shouldn't Mama be wailing or Grace swearing she had no idea that Hope had left in the dead of night? Shouldn't

Quent be ranting about honor or behavior or something like that?

She closed her eyes, took a steadying breath, and then stepped into the yellow Kilworth parlor. Then her mouth fell open. What in the world was *Danby* doing here?

The duke sat in a high-back chair as though he was holding court, while Thad, a couple she wasn't familiar with, and the rest of her family were scattered about he room, every one of them holding their tongues. In all her days, she'd never seen her mother be so quiet for so long. Of course, the duke terrified Mama.

"Sorry to keep you waiting," she said softly.

Thad leapt to his feet while Danby, Quent and Mr. Wright all pushed out of their seats.

"I'd wait for you forever," Thad said and crossed the room to take her hands in his.

Of course he hadn't even waited until they were married to *have* her, and the memory of their morning spent in his bed washed over Hope. She was fairly certain she was blushing to her roots.

"Shall we get on with this?" The Duke of Danby tapped his cane against the floor. "I don't have all day."

The awful duke. At least after she and Thad married, she'd never have to worry about what His Grace might or might not do in regards to her future. She pitied Patience living so close to the man in Yorkshire.

"I'm ready." Thad smiled down at her. "Are you?"

She nodded in response. She didn't think she'd ever been more ready for anything in all her life.

Thad led her toward the large window and then looked back at Mr. Wright. "Will this be all right?"

"It'll be just fine," the man replied, coming to stand near them with his bible in his hand.

Quent came up to stand beside Hope and whispered in

her ear, "Your buttons are off. Best not let Kilworth dress you in the future."

She sucked in a breath and her cheeks stung. How off were her buttons? "I don't know what you mean," she lied.

But her brother only shook his head. "It's a good thing you're marrying the man," he said only loud enough for her, and possibly Thad, to hear.

Mr. Wright cleared his throat. "Proverbs 5:18. *May your fountain be blessed, and may you—*"

"If we wanted a sermon, Mr. Wright, we would be at services on Sunday," the duke complained. "Do get on with it."

The man's eyes widened in shock. "Of course, Your Grace." Then he quickly shut his bible. "Um, do you, Thaddeus Alan Baxter, take Hope Elizabeth Post to have and to hold from this day forward, for better, for worse, for richer, for poorer, in sickness or in health, to love and to cherish 'til death do you part?"

Thad smiled down at Hope and her breath nearly caught in her throat. "I do."

She took a breath as Mr. Wright turned his attention to her.

"And do you, Hope Elizabeth Post take Thaddeus Alan Baxter to have and to hold from this day forward, for better, for worse, for richer, for poorer, in sickness or in health, to love, honor, and obey 'til death do you part?"

She nodded and whispered, "I do."

Mr. Wright frowned. "I don't suppose you have a ring, my lord?"

But Thad reached inside his pocket and retrieved a beautiful emerald ring surrounded by the prettiest diamonds. "It was my grandmother's," he said softly. "If it doesn't fit…"

And it *was* a tiny bit big, but he slid it onto Hope's finger, and it sparkled in the sunlight pouring in through the window. "It's beautiful."

"It pales in comparison to *you*, Lady Kilworth."

Lady Kilworth. She was Lady Kilworth. It was somewhat surreal as she'd always thought she would be Lady Kilworth, only to a different earl. But Thad…Well, Thad wasn't Henry. He was so much better in every way, which Hope would have never thought possible, and yet it was.

"You may now kiss your bride," Mr. Wright said.

Thad released Hope's hands, cupped her face and pressed the gentlest of kisses to her lips.

∼

It was a relief when Quentin Post slapped a hand to Thad's back and welcomed him into the family. It was a relief when Lady Bradenham's lips actually cracked a smile as she congratulated Hope on her fine match, and when Sarah promised to invite Hope to tea later in the week. But the biggest relief was when the Duke of Danby finally left Baxter House for parts unknown.

What a day it had been. The longest one Thad could remember living through, and he hoped he never forgot even a moment of it.

As soon as her family and his had finally returned to their own homes, Hope pushed up on her tiptoes and pressed a kiss to Thad's lips. "Do you know what I'd like to do now?" She batted her lashes at him.

He would like to return to his chambers with her, but he had a feeling she was going to say something else. "What would you like to do now?"

Her grin lit up the parlor. "Go for a spirited ride along the Bath Road."

He should have known. "As luck would have it, my phaeton was returned to me yesterday."

Hope's green eyes sparkled with joy. "And you really don't mind taking me?"

There were so many places he'd like to *take* her, but that wasn't what she meant. And that reckless spirit he loved so much about her was in full form right then. "It'll be my greatest pleasure…at least until we come home and retire for the night."

ABOUT AVA STONE

Ava Stone is a USA Today bestselling author of Regency historical romance and college age New Adult romance. Whether in the 19th Century or the 21st, her books explore deep themes but with a light touch. A single mother, Ava lives outside Raleigh NC, but she travels extensively, always looking for inspiration for new stories and characters in the various locales she visits.

You can subscribe to Ava's newsletter HERE.

Connect With Ava Stone
www.avastoneauthor.com
ava@avastoneauthor.com

ALSO BY AVA STONE

REGENCY SEASONS SERIES

A Counterfeit Christmas Summons
By Any Other Name
My Lord Hercules
A Bit of Mistletoe
The Lady Vanishes
Prelude to a Haunted Evening
The Lady Unmasked
Lady Patience's Christmas Kitten
Lady Hope's Dashing Devil
Lady Grace's Husband Hunt

THE SCANDALOUS SERIES

A Scandalous Wife
A Scandalous Charade
A Scandalous Secret
A Scandalous Pursuit
A Scandalous Past
My Favorite Major
The English Lieutenant's Lady
To Catch a Captain
Encounter With an Adventurer
In The Stars

Promises Made
A Scandalous Deception
A Scandalous Ruse
A Scandalous Vow